Nurse Camilla's Love

*Also by Colleen L. Reece
in Large Print:*

A Girl Called Cricket
Ballad for Nurse Lark
Belated Follower
Come Home, Nurse Jenny
Mysterious Monday
Nurse Autumn's Secret Love
The Hills of Hope
Thursday Trials
Trouble on Tuesday
Wednesday Witness
Yellowstone Park Nurse

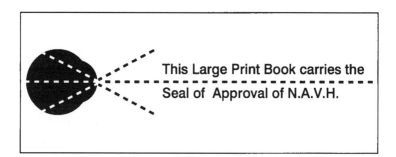

This Large Print Book carries the
Seal of Approval of N.A.V.H.

NURSE CAMILLA'S LOVE

Colleen L. Reece

Thorndike Press • Waterville, Maine

Published in 2001 by arrangement with Colleen L. Reece.

Thorndike Press Large Print Candlelight Series.

The tree indicium is a trademark of Thorndike Press.

The text of this Large Print edition is unabridged.
Other aspects of the book may vary from the original edition.

Set in 16 pt. Plantin by Myrna S. Raven.

Printed in the United States on permanent paper.

Library of Congress Cataloging-in-Publication Data

Reece, Colleen L.
    Nurse Camilla's love / Colleen L. Reece.
        p. cm.
    ISBN 0-7862-3621-3 (lg. print : hc : alk. paper)
    1. Nurses — Fiction. 2. Psychiatrists — Fiction.
  3. Accident victims — Fiction. 4. Large type books.
  I. Title.
PS3568.E3646 N86 2001
  813'.54—dc21
                                                  2001041550

Nurse Camilla's Love

PROLOGUE

It was a hospital-room scene Camilla would never forget — never — even though no one was aware of her presence.

"What are *you* doing here?" the man in bed furiously demanded of another man, who had just entered the dimly lit room.

The late-night visitor had a heavily bandaged head. That was all the girl could see of him from her hiding place. She herself had sneaked into the room earlier, unnoticed by anyone.

"I had to come, sir." Something in the second man's voice stilled the anger on the lips of the bedridden man. The visitor stepped closer to the bed, clutching the edge of it with tense white fingers. "Captain Montgomery, can you ever forgive me?"

"Forgive!" The captain's bitter word cut through the visitor's determination to win a personal pardon. "Forgive you for putting me in a wheelchair for the rest of my life?"

The second man flinched but held his ground. "I was drunk, sir."

"I know. I was there, remember?"

"If only you hadn't been!" There was

agony in the visitor's voice. "If you had just left me alone. Better for me to die than for you to be crippled!"

The young man's deep sincerity reached Jim Montgomery more than anything else could have done. But suddenly he was tired. He didn't want to talk to this man. The hatred was almost gone. Now all Jim wanted to do was rest.

And yet the sense of responsibility that had caused him as C.O. — commanding officer — to check out his men on their return from the P.O.W. camp wouldn't let him leave it there.

He shivered, remembering how happy they'd all been. Skin and bones, but happy to be free from the Viet Cong. They'd hit the States, been hospitalized for a time, then met for a final farewell party. During the months they'd spent crammed together in that prison camp they'd grown to be brothers, fighting insanity as well as the indignities and hardships. And now they would have one final farewell.

The man — no, boy — before Jim had been the loudest, the gladdest to be back in the States. He was younger than the rest of them and had come from a home rich in money, poor in family ties.

Yet he'd been glad to be at the farewell

8

party. His eyes had brimmed as he lifted his glass, saying, "To the future!" It wasn't the first glass he'd lifted that night. He seemed anxious to annihilate the past with liquor. "Captain, to you!"

Jim lifted his own glass, filled with ginger ale. He hated booze. He knew what it could do to people. "Haven't you had about enough?" he'd asked.

"No, sir!" The young man had another drink, then another. Finally, he said, "Here's to everybody!" He threw his glass toward the window. And by freakish chance it knocked a candle from the table into the sheer curtains. In moments they were blazing.

"Come on. We have to get out of here!" Jim was the only one sober enough to see the extent of the danger. Some of the others were ineffectually trying to smother the fire. By pushing and shoving, Jim got them downstairs and outside in the cold air and counted. One was missing.

"Don't go back, Captain!" The cry didn't stop him. He was inside the house, groping through the smoke and flames to find the man who had inadvertently ended their celebration in fire. Where was he? Step by step, Jim retraced the route until he found his man, huddled on the floor upstairs, knocked out by a great chunk of plaster.

With an ease born of his long-ago training, he hoisted his burden to his shoulders and staggered down the stairs — while the flames grew more menacing — and outside. He dropped his burden, stumbling over the doorsill.

"Captain!" The cry mingled with a great crash.

Jim glanced up, horrified, struggling to get to his feet. He could see his men running toward him, sobered by the cold night air and the flames. It was too late. With a mighty crash the entire doorway fell, bathing the captain in fire. . . .

Jim Montgomery forced himself back to the present. Would he never forget those moments? He could see them reflected in the eyes of his visitor. How much more agonizing they must be to him!

Never in his life had Jim played the part of C.O. better than he did now. Despite the difficulty of moving, he drew himself up as best he could. "What would you give to make restitution for your drunken act?" he asked the second man.

"My life." It was said simply, without dramatics.

"That wouldn't do me any good. But

10

there is a way." Jim paused, swallowing hard. "Would you be willing to spend the rest of your life paying for my being crippled?"

The bandaged man before him could only nod.

"You know," Jim said, "I was almost through my medical training when I enlisted."

Another nod.

"I know a good deal about you, too," Jim went on. "I know you could be a good doctor. I know you have the guts and intelligence to do it, if you want to badly enough. I also know you were kicked out of medical school for refusing to take your work seriously."

The young man's face was parchment color in the dim light. Everything Captain Montgomery was saying was true. How long ago and faraway it all seemed. Now, even the prison camp paled into insignificance beside the monstrous accident. The man in the bed had risked his life, lost his ability to walk, because he himself had lain in a drunken stupor, knocked out during a fire he had caused!

"When I get out of here, I intend to finish my training," the captain said. "But I'll never be able to make my dream come true.

I had planned to devote my life and career to working in various Veterans' Administration hospitals. You saw those men coming home from Vietnam. In addition to all the other problems from other wars, this time there's the drug problem. There's also the bitterness coming from fighting a war many Americans feel to be unjust. Other veterans came home heroes. Us? There are those who think we're chumps.

"I don't know how much I'll be able to do," the captain continued. "Not surgery. I won't be able to stand on my feet. But I will do something. As for you, if you're really willing to pay, go back and finish your training! Tell the V.A. of your past training, everything. Then show them you're going to be the best doctor who ever lived. When you're through, go to the veterans' hospitals. Work with those who served. Make my dream come true."

For the first time Captain Jim Montgomery's studied calm threatened to break. "If you feel responsible for these" — he brought his hands down hard on the worthless legs — "replace them with your own health and strength."

There was silence in the room. Then, before Jim's eyes, the young man who had always seemed a boy to him straightened. His face was still dead white. But there was a glorified look about him.

Awkwardly the young man brought his hand to his bandaged head in a full salute. "Yes, sir." He turned and marched from the room.

Jim Montgomery sank back on the pillows, spent. What had he done? He had opened up his secret dream and asked another man to fulfill it. He closed his eyes. It was too much. No one in the world could replace another, could make a personal dream come true. Yet something in the boy who had become a man seemed to deny that last thought.

If he did it, it would be the finest thing in the world. It would be a sacrifice. But he would end up saving himself from being "just another rich man's son."

Jim yawned. The sleeping pill that had not taken effect earlier now soothed him. In moments, he was asleep, too tired to even consider the matter any longer.

Earlier, neither Captain Montgomery nor his visitor had noticed the slight movement of the screen beside the bed. Neither of them had seen the quick opening and closing of the adjoining bathroom door, with only a crack to betray the occupant inside. They had not seen the frail, thin teenage girl who huddled behind the door, determined to be near Jim if needed.

Camilla had not meant to eavesdrop. She had only wanted to be by the man who had meant so much in her life. As the little drama had unfolded, she'd found herself hot and cold by turns. And she had felt a terrible hatred for the young visitor with the bandaged head. She had not seen his face. From her sheltered position, she had only seen his general shape — tall, huddled over from the weight of the remorse he carried. His voice had been muffled, masked by emotion. She probably wouldn't recognize it again if she heard it.

When Captain Montgomery had given the young man his challenge, she had been thrilled. Yet she still felt resentment toward the younger soldier. She felt something else, too — a desire to help the captain in her own way.

She was young in years, still in her teens, yet why couldn't she become a nurse?

Perhaps the soldier would in time forget or go on to be something else. She would not forget.

Only after Jim fell asleep did the bathroom door open fully as the slight figure stepped into view.

For a moment Camilla looked down at

the sleeping man. And she whispered, "Yes, Captain. I'll remember."

Then she slipped back into the white-tiled lavatory. Seconds later, Camilla's ghostly figure slipped through the empty room on the other side of the bathroom, then into the hall. She checked for medical personnel and, seeing none, made her way outside. No one need know of the two visitors to Captain Jim Montgomery except those whose lives would be changed by the challenge he had issued. One challenge, two acceptances.

Later that night, while Jim slept the healing sleep his body needed, a wide-eyed girl and a young soldier who had forever left childhood behind him lay sleepless, planning for futures to fulfill their promises to a crippled captain.

Chapter 1

"Coming, Camilla?"

The dark-eyed girl by the mirror pulled the hairbrush through her long dark hair a final time, checked her lipstick, and hurried to the hall. "Ready." Her throat tightened as she saw the eagerness in her stepbrother's face. Even in a wheelchair Jim was the best-looking man she knew. Was that why, all these years, no one had attracted more than passing interest from her?

"You're staring at me as if you've never seen me before," he accused, wheeling himself outside. His blue eyes twinkled above the immaculate white doctor's tunic he wore. His unruly sandy hair lay down for once.

Camilla swallowed hard and forced a smile. "Maybe I haven't. At least I've never seen you so on the crest of a wave." She flicked a disdainful finger. "Of course, just because the new veterans' hospital has been completed here in Auburn, and you've been named hospital director, and it's to be dedicated today, and your sister has a brand new job as head nurse on ward 8, that couldn't have anything to do with it, could it?"

"Perhaps." His white teeth flashed. "You realize that after today I'll be Dr. Montgomery to you and you'll be Miss Clark to me at the hospital." He deliberately increased his drawl. "After all, there'll be no favoritism shown to the head nurse on ward 8 because of family ties."

"Nut!" The gladness in her voice outshone even her sparkling eyes. It had been a long struggle to get Jim to this point. He had spent years to overcome his handicap, more time finishing his medical training and being accepted as a good doctor. Was it in spite of, or because of, the wheelchair he had struggled so hard? Well, now was not the time for introspection.

"May I?" She proudly touched his hand. Strong, brown, hard. The result of an intense desire to make life all it could be.

"It's still hard to believe it's really true," Camilla said, following Jim's pointing finger. They were facing the hospital now, the brand new hospital for which they had waited so long. Jim's eyes greedily took in every shrub and tree planted to enhance the entrance. The hospital director's own house was directly across the parklike driveway, a charming four-bedroom ranch-style place. It was perfect for them, close enough to be convenient for Jim, just far enough away

17

from the hospital to give a feeling of privacy.

"Look, Jim!" Camilla raised her face to the sky. The hospital had been built so that Mt. Rainier could be seen directly behind it. Its snowcapped crown rested against the blue sky, giving a feeling of security.

"I never really thought it would happen," Jim confessed as they neared the front doors of the hospital. They were glass, sparkling clean, giving a glimpse of many potted plants in the foyer.

The local merchants had done themselves proud in providing flowers for opening day. Entering the hospital was like stepping into a garden. Or a funeral parlor. Camilla suppressed a laugh. Trust her to think of something like that!

The dedication service was to be held in the main patients' dining room. Slowly, gradually, people began filing in. Jim had wanted to be there early, seated on the platform when the crowds arrived. The governor was there, the mayor, all the usual dignitaries. Yet Jim Montgomery in his simple white tunic overshadowed them all.

There wasn't one person present who didn't know of his fight to have the hospital built in Auburn. He had stormed the fortresses when he heard of a new veterans' hospital planned for Seattle.

18

"Not Seattle," he had cried to any official who would listen. "They already have a veterans' hospital. Put it outside Auburn. Put it where there is some scenery to look at instead of concrete streets."

There had been those who listened. Now it was real. If government hospitals were named after those who worked for them, it would have been called the JIM MONT-GOMERY HOSPITAL. As it was, the simple stone sign proclaimed it as the AUBURN VETERANS' HOSPITAL.

Somewhere between the mayor's and the governor's speeches, Camilla's attention wandered. She had been watching Jim, as she'd done for the last several years. As a head nurse she was merely one of the crowd, free to settle back and observe.

Yet somehow the scene, intense as it was, faded from her vision to be replaced by other scenes from the past. She had been not quite five when her widowed mother married Fred Montgomery.

Her own father had died when she was a baby. Fred's wife had been killed in a car wreck years before. They became a family, along with Fred's sixteen-year-old son, Jim.

Despite the tremendous age difference, a great love grew between the little girl and her "big brother." He never was too busy to play

19

with her or take her places. As she grew into adolescence, he was the one who helped the gawky, shy girl see herself as a real person.

When he left his medical studies to serve in the armed forces during the Vietnam War, she cried buckets and faithfully wrote him. The blackest day in her life was the day the family learned that Jim was believed to be a P.O.W. By contrast, the happiest day was the day he was released.

There was one memory Camilla skimmed over. Was it because she never should have been in his hospital room on a certain fateful night? Her mother and stepfather never knew. She'd managed, with the aid of a sturdy tree trunk near her window, to slip out of the house. Later, she'd climbed back to her room the same way.

She hadn't forgotten the vow she'd made. When Jim got home from the hospital, she'd casually announced, "I'm going to be a nurse someday."

Her family didn't know how intensely she had studied during the rest of high school, or how, when she entered nurse's training, she was far ahead of the rest of her class.

Training had been everything she looked forward to, but in her final year, her mother and stepfather were killed in a plane crash.

She would never forget that time, how

she'd wanted to drop training and start supporting herself.

"No!" Jim had insisted. "You finish that training. We're all that's left, Camilla. We have to stick together."

Together. The word filled Camilla's heart as she saw Jim take the microphone now. They had been together and would stay that way.

Once Jim had asked curiously, "No sweethearts, Cam? I know the guys must be interested."

"No one special. I've been too busy."

His reply was soft. "Don't ever let me stand in your way."

"Who, me?" She made her laugh bright. "I have a feeling when Mr. Right comes along, nothing on earth will stand in the way. You know how headstrong I am!"

"Mr. Right! That dates you. No wonder you scare the guys off! That idea is straight out of yesterday."

"So what? Don't you feel the same way?" Her hand flew to her lips, horrified at what she'd said.

"Don't worry about it, Cam. I've already faced the fact I'll never marry. But I don't want to be a millstone around your neck."

"I could just marry you myself. We're not really sister and brother, you know."

His face turned white. He was angrier than she'd ever seen him. "Don't be completely stupid! You're my sister." Seeing the stricken look on her face, he laughed a little unconvincingly. "Besides, if I ever *did* want to marry, it wouldn't be an icicle like you — I'd want someone who was mushy over me."

It was the last time they discussed marriage. Time enough to think about that in the future.

Meanwhile, Jim had been overjoyed to find that Camilla fully intended to work in veterans' hospitals. "It's not just because of me?" he asked.

This time it was her turn to tease. "Of course not. Think of all the wonderful opportunities I'll have to meet men!"

He had peered at her over his glasses, then chuckled and dropped the subject.

Jim was speaking now. "This is a day I — we have all looked forward to for a long time. As hospital director I pledge to give my best to every patient and employee. I promise you that if I ever feel someone else can step in and do a better job, I'll hand in my resignation."

The storm of applause held elements of protest. Everyone in Auburn knew of Jim Montgomery's fights — his private battle to overcome his handicap and his battle for this hospital. Now in a body they stood, giving tribute to one who richly deserved their praise.

"Yes, sir, I'll do my best!" Jim was now responding to the mayor.

But in a flash Camilla's mind fled to the past once more.

She saw herself cowering, hidden in the precarious safety of the hospital bathroom adjoining Jim's room. She saw a young soldier with a bandaged head. What had happened to him? Had he gone on to become a doctor? Would she ever be able to forgive him? What would she do if she met this man who had put her brother in that wheelchair? Rush at him like some old-fashioned heroine, shouting, "You wronged my brother!"?

She thought: *I hope, wherever he is, he hears on the news or reads in the paper what Jim has done with his life. I hope that boy — no, man — really did go on to become a doctor.* The little prayer winged upward even as she stood with the rest of the crowd for "The Star Spangled Banner." It was over, the dedication. Now it was time to start a new and different part of her life.

"You know, Jim, I still can't believe how

efficient this hospital plant is," Camilla said. "Why, it's a little village all its own." They were finishing dinner in their own kitchen. When they were both working they'd eat in the staff dining room, but in the meantime Camilla liked to cook at home.

"That's right. We're completely self-sufficient. We have our own laundry. Lighting system for emergencies. Food storage. Boiler plant. Shops — mechanical, electrical, plumbing, carpenter repair. Library. Chapel. And a million other things."

"I still find it hard to grasp," she said. "It impresses me to be part of this whole thing."

"It should, Cam. I feel rehabilitating servicemen and women and caring for them is one of the most important jobs in the world."

"Don't forget the domiciliary wards." She sighed. "Can you imagine being an incapacitated veteran and having nowhere else to live except in a domiciliary ward?"

"It might not be so bad. All food and medical care are provided. We try to use color to play down the hospital atmosphere. The ones who are well enough can eat in the patients' dining room if they choose. There is the recreation room, movies, chapel, the library."

"I know, but still." She was unconvinced.

"It's such a tragic thing. Why, the time I was working in the Seattle V.A. hospital some of the domiciliary patients were practically helpless and never had one visitor!"

"Who would visit me if I didn't have you and I were totally incapacitated and lived in the hospital?" Quick as a flash Jim added, "I retract that statement. What a morbid, self-pitying comment!" Then he said, "Hey, Cam, think of all the experience you'll get. Even though you're head nurse on ward 8 right now, later maybe you'll want to try some of the other wards. We sure have everything to offer — including psychiatric care."

"The only things we don't have are obstetrics and pediatrics," she said.

"Leave it to you. I can just see you, Cam." He mimicked a young nurse rolling her eyes, speaking with falsetto voice. "But, Mr. Hospital Director, no *babies?*"

"You really are a nut." She began to clear the table. "Jim, I know it's going to sound dumb, but — there won't be any talk about our living here, will there?"

"Why should there be?" His blue eyes behind the glasses were surprised.

"Well, I really am not your sister, and —"

"No one knows that, Cam. As far as everyone is concerned, we're brother and

25

sister. So we have different last names. That's not uncommon, not with all the divorces there are." He noted the little scowl between her brows. "I can't imagine anyone having anything to say, especially when I'm in a wheelchair. If they do, I'll see it's taken care of."

"Thanks, Jim. I really didn't want to bring it up, but you know how people can be sometimes."

"Sure, Cam. If anyone says anything, I'll just tell them you're my nurse and that will take care of it!" He wheeled himself into the living room. "Get your dishes done and come watch a program with me, will you?"

It was good to hear him so cheerful, but Camilla couldn't let things stay as they were. Somehow the dedication had opened up all kinds of memories.

When she finished the kitchen work and went to the living room, Jim looked up from the TV set. "This isn't too good. Turn it off, will you, Cam? We can watch something later."

Her heart was thumping. "Jim, could we talk?" Seeing his surprise, she added, "About the past, I mean."

Instantly his face was closed against her. "There's nothing to say."

She tried to break through the invisible

26

barrier formed in that moment. "Yes, there is. I have to ask — what happened to Alice Shannon?" She didn't think he would answer.

But he said, "When I was in the accident, I told her everything was off. I didn't want to see her again." He ignored Camilla's gasp. "I've never spoken of it since, but I'll tell you now. Then I won't talk about it again. We were engaged, you knew that."

He didn't see her nod. "All during my years in Vietnam, during the P.O.W. days, I kept Alice in my mind and heart." His voice was husky. "I could hardly wait to get back, to finish my training. She had completed her nurse's training and degree and was working, saving for our future. She wanted to be ready with a little backlog when I was a full-fledged doctor.

"Everything was fine — until the fire." His voice was expressionless, but Camilla could see the pain in his eyes. So he had not forgotten, even after all these years. "She came to the hospital. I told her I didn't want to see her again. She went away."

"You mean to say you didn't even give her a choice?" Camilla could hardly believe her ears. "You didn't ask her how *she* felt?"

"And have her assure me she still loved me, it wouldn't make any difference?" His eyes were blazing. "I didn't want her pity. She was the kind of woman who would have stuck if it killed her. Well, that wasn't for me. I want no one's pity."

"What about her love?"

"Under the circumstances, that was hardly the issue." He rolled his chair across the room and turned on the TV, a signal the conversation was over.

But long after Camilla had gone to bed that night, she could hear him tossing and turning. How unfair of him not to give Alice a choice in the decision! To merely announce it was all off.

Had she been wrong to make him discuss it? Her training told her even his success with the new Auburn Veterans' Hospital would not replace the therapeutic value of bringing into the open some of the past wounds Jim had experienced, instead of hiding them forever.

Until he could completely face the past, he could never make the present and future whole. Perhaps it was cruel to force issues. Yet often the seeming cruelty of the surgeon's knife was the only thing that could cure.

I wonder — where is Alice Shannon now? Camilla thought. *Did she marry? I wonder if I could find her. But if I did, would Jim ever forgive me?*

Chapter 2

Jim Montgomery frowned at the letter lying on his desk. It had come like a wraith from the past, bringing back days he'd put aside forever. The question was, what should he do about it?

He reread the doctor's glowing praise for the young man who was being considered as head of the psychiatric ward of his hospital. "Although fairly young in experience . . . outstanding candidate . . . shows promise of being one of the best in the country."

He automatically dropped his hand over the letter as Camilla entered. How good she looked in her white uniform! She positively glowed. Even in the short months since the hospital had opened, she had made a real place for herself. Everyone from the cook to the chief of staff had learned to know her and her enthusiasm for her work.

Sometimes Jim had to "call her off," in order to see that she got enough rest. When one of her guys, as she called all the ward 8 patients, was involved, she'd work all night.

"Hail and farewell, boss!" She dropped into a chair, grinning. "How come the royal invitation to your honorable office?"

His lips curved in an answering smile. For a moment an image of the scrawny kid she'd been rose to blur his vision, to be replaced by Camilla in person.

"Glad you're properly impressed by the honor." He made a quick decision, pushing the pages on his desk across to her. Camilla's judgment was excellent. Besides, no one would ever know he'd shown her the credentials.

"What do you think?"

She read them through — the letter and the recommendations from other doctors throughout the country. The doctors from the candidate's medical school and training hospital, then the ones from doctors at hospitals where he'd worked. There was even a newspaper story with a picture.

"Sounds good. Maybe he's just the man we need." Her look was level. "Why? Do you think there's something fishy?"

"No. Just wanted your opinion."

Not by word or look did Camilla show her surprise. He'd never asked before. Was he tired? Was the hospital directorship getting him down? No, she answered her own question. He'd never looked better.

"My opinion is that we'll be lucky to get him," she said. "Better write right away. We really need a good psychiatric ward doctor. The ones who are working there are fine, but they need a strong director." She looked at the newspaper clipping. "Marc Butler. Dark hair, dark eyes. Hmmm, good-looking." A little frown crossed her face. "Has he ever been here? He looks familiar."

"You wouldn't know him." Jim leaned back. "All right. If you've given him the once-over, I'll get a letter out right away."

"Doesn't personnel usually handle all that?"

There was a curious smile on her brother's face. "I think in this case it would be warmer if I extended the invitation to visit us and be interviewed myself."

"Boy, he gets the royal treatment, too, huh?" she teased. "On the other hand, if he lives up to his advance publicity, it will be worth it." Camilla stepped through the door he pushed aside. But she failed to hear him mutter, "I hope so."

When Marc Butler received the letter, he couldn't believe it. He had been recommended for a position he hadn't even applied for. The letter said:

Dear Dr. Butler,

It has come to my attention you are making a name for yourself in the world of psychiatric medicine, especially in working with veterans and their special problems.

I have taken the trouble to look up your references and find them excellent. As I am sure you know, we now have a brand new veterans' hospital here in Auburn, Washington. It has been staffed with experts in every field, men and women who are truly skilled and dedicated.

There is an opening for that kind of doctor to head up our psychiatric ward. If you are interested, I would appreciate hearing from you at your earliest convenience.

I trust you will give this your full consideration.

Sincerely yours,
James Montgomery, M.D.

What a plum! To be offered such a position over many other qualified doctors. Should he consider it? It would mean leaving his present position, but he had never intended to stay there forever.

What would it be like to work for James Montgomery? The world of the veterans' hospitals buzzed with the work he was doing, how he'd fought tooth and nail to get that hospital built in Auburn.

It couldn't be an easy job to run such a hospital. And even in the few months the hospital had been open, it had been filled with patients. Marc had made it a point to keep track of what was happening. The V.A. hospitals in both Seattle and Vancouver had sent excess patients to Auburn.

What a challenge! Was he a big enough man to take it? For one moment the words on the letter blurred, to be replaced by the image of himself, years earlier, promising, "I'd do anything." Now Marc Butler had that chance. His heart leaped. He'd do it.

Anticipation mingled with regret as he told his own chief of staff about the offer, noting how the chief rejoiced for him even while protesting he couldn't be spared.

"Well, at least tell them you can't start work for a month or so. Not that we can replace you in that time, but at least maybe we can adjust."

Marc's telegram to Auburn was short and to the point: FLYING IN ON UNITED FRIDAY NIGHT. ARRIVAL TIME 9:00 P.M.

The answer was equally brief: YOU WILL BE MET. WAIT UNDER CLOCK AT UNITED TICKETS.

33

★ ★ ★

It was late Thursday afternoon when the call came. "Miss Clark, Dr. Montgomery wants you to report to his office as soon as you can get away."

Automatically Camilla checked the time. Only five minutes until the end of her shift. "All right, Susan. I'm all through here anyway."

What could Jim want? He almost never called her to his office. As she glided down the long hall in the rapid walk that covered the distance without giving a feeling of haste, a strange premonition swept over her.

"What's wrong?" she demanded, stepping into his office.

"I've been called to Washington, D.C., for a special V.A. meeting this next week. I have to leave tomorrow afternoon."

"So?" Her face was proud. "What does Washington need you for?"

"They're calling hospital directors from several western states. There are some new directives being issued and we're to be briefed. One of the hospitals in California that housed domiciliary patients is unsafe, the result of various minor earthquakes. They need to be evacuated. We'll be getting our domiciliary ward filled up."

"The trip will do you good."

He was impatient. "Sure, that's no problem. What is a problem is that Dr. Butler's coming in on the plane tomorrow night. You'll have to meet him, show him around. He'd only planned to stay for the weekend, but you'll have to get him to stay until next Thursday. I'll be back Wednesday night."

"But what am I supposed to do with him when I'm on duty?"

"Camilla, I'm sure your ward is run well enough to spare you for a few days." He was already reaching for the phone. "Operator, I want an outside line."

In a daze Camilla heard only parts of his conversation. *She* was supposed to show him around? Why not one of the other doctors? For a moment she thought of protesting, then thought, *This isn't a suggestion from Jim. It's an order from the hospital director. He knows what's best for the hospital.*

Her meditations were interrupted by Jim.

"Good. I was able to get Marc Butler and explain. Now, Camilla, this is what you need to do . . ." He was off on a direct track, outlining how she'd introduce Dr. Butler to the various doctors, department heads, and so forth. "Let him wander around on his own part of the time, too," Jim finished.

"But where will he stay?" Camilla asked.

For a moment Jim stared at her. Then he dialed the chief of staff's office. "I need a favor. A candidate for the position in the psychiatry ward's coming in. And I have to be gone. Can you take him in?" In another moment he had hung up. "Simple, see?"

"Boy," she scoffed, "what a soft job you have! Just sit here and pull strings. Call someone and presto! Thy will be done!"

"You're a good sport, Cam. Besides, as you said, he's dark and handsome. Who knows? Maybe you'll even enjoy your public relations duties."

She matched his tone. "Sure. I'll probably even fall in love with him."

"Never!"

Camilla was startled by the vehemence in his voice. But before she could question Jim, his phone rang again. He motioned to the door. "Go on ahead. Can we eat at home tonight? I'd like to fill you in some more." He turned to the call, leaving Camilla to stare at him. Then she slowly turned and walked out the door, still wondering.

My heavens, but he had been upset by her silly comment! Why?

But when he arrived home, Jim was as usual. They ate the broiled steaks, tossed salad, and rolls she'd fixed, enjoying the unexpected free time together.

"Should do more of this," Jim sighed. "But with our schedules, it's not practical." He eyed Camilla contentedly. "You've managed to feed the beast, now let's talk."

"We'd better pack while we talk." She led the way to his room, taking down a suitcase from the hall closet on the way. Her hands folded garments even as he explained more to her what to do with Dr. Butler.

"Camilla, I think what you said earlier is right."

Her hands froze. What comment was that?

He went on. "If we can get Dr. Butler we'll be lucky. It's going to be up to you to sell him on Auburn."

"Me!" Her gasp was surprised. "I don't even know the man."

"Neither does anyone else here. Just stick close and answer questions, then give him time to wander around. Be sure to meet him for meals and see that he meets people."

"Yes, Dr. Montgomery. As you say, Dr. Montgomery." She abandoned her sarcasm. "It means a lot to you for him to accept the job, doesn't it, Jim?"

"More than you'll ever know." His quiet voice said a great deal.

If Camilla had not been so preoccupied with her own upcoming duties, she might have noticed it more. As it was, she thought how the addition of Dr. Butler would complete the full staff, how it would relieve some of the strain for Jim.

There was a mist in her eyes as she watched Jim being helped into the hospital car the next day. Once he was at the airport, he would roll up the ramp, and when he reached Washington, D.C., he would be met. Silly for her to feel overly protective, as if a small child was being sent off alone to fend for itself.

This would probably be the first of many trips for Jim. She needn't feel so lost, alone. And Jim looked so gallant, waving to her from the car window.

She swallowed hard and smiled, never knowing her feelings were mirrored in her face for Jim to see. He could feel some of her excitement and concern. It was the first time they'd really be apart since she had come to work in Auburn.

Camilla had never looked lovelier than she did in the scarlet pants outfit she chose to wear for her first meeting with Dr. Butler. Her dark hair shone from brushing. The white blouse just visible beneath her red jacket was sparkling and lacy.

Jim had said to make a good impression. Well, she would. If being perfectly groomed could help get the kind of doctor they wanted, that's what she'd be! She laughed at her own nonsense. She couldn't stand to be other than well-groomed. It was second nature to her.

The plane was on time. Camilla made her way toward the meeting place, the clock at United Tickets. Marc Butler was there before her. As she approached, she noticed how quietly he stood. He was clearly recognizable from his newspaper picture.

"Dr. Butler?"

He looked at her in surprise. Seconds before, he had noticed this young woman crossing the terminal, taking in her lovely face and figure. He had thought, *I've never seen a more beautiful woman.* Now she was speaking to him.

"Dr. Butler? I'm Camilla Clark from the hospital."

"How lucky can a doctor get?" His spontaneous tribute, followed by a wide grin, brought color to her skin.

She looked at him suspiciously for a moment. Was he a wolf? But the frankness of his face stilled the suspicion. She laughed. "With that opening, we should get on well together."

As she led the way to pick up his luggage, he noticed she was tall, slender. Her dark hair and eyes were replicas of his own. There was a dimple in the otherwise firm chin, and laughter lurked in the dark eyes, ready to spill over.

Marc Butler had never felt quite like this on meeting a strange woman. What was it about her? His scrutiny brought out that her ravishing beauty was partly an illusion. Oh, she was very pretty, to be sure. But he had seen many women with more perfect features. Yet Camilla Clark had a certain air about her, giving an impression of warmth, concern, and fearlessness.

At the luggage carousel he turned from her to get his suitcase. When he turned back, he noticed she had brushed a hand over her eyes, as if to dispel some unwanted shadow. "Are you all right?"

Camilla nodded, but didn't explain. What was there to explain? An unaccountable sense of familiarity? Ridiculous! Jim had said she didn't know this man. Red flags of color waved in her cheeks even as she led him to the parked car.

Why was he affecting her so strangely? She knew, as if it were absolute truth, Marc Butler would be more in her life than just a casual acquaintance. The next minute she scoffed. He was probably married!

This time Camilla's good sense settled her down. "Did you have dinner?" she asked.

"No. It wasn't a dinner flight. I'd meant to eat before I went to the airport, but got tied up." There was something schoolboyish in his tone. "Could you, that is, would it be imposing on you to ask you to have a snack with me?"

"Not at all." She considered. "Do you like fish?"

"I love it!"

She smiled at his fervent answer. "Good. There's a Sea Galley restaurant practically on the way home. They have a good variety and a salad bar that's out of this world."

In spite of the many times Camilla had been out to dinner with attractive men, this time was different. They had to wait at the restaurant: it was popular and crowded. It didn't seem to bother Marc in the least.

There was one awkward moment after the hostess asked, "Would you care for cocktails at the bar?"

Camilla hesitated. She never drank. Her parents had raised her to leave alcohol alone. But perhaps Dr. Butler would want a drink.

"Not me. I don't drink." The doctor's

voice was almost curt.

"I don't, either." Camilla smiled at the hostess, then at Marc. Silly for that glad little feeling to come up inside her. When the hostess had gone, she asked idly, "How did you manage to get through medical school without drinking?"

She wasn't prepared for the white look of suffering that filled his face. For a moment she didn't know if he was going to answer. To fill in the pause, she added, "That's really none of my business. I don't know why I asked."

"I'd like you to know. A long time ago I did something when I had been drinking that resulted in a tragedy. It was the last drink I ever took — or ever will take."

The emotion-filled moment was broken by the hostess beckoning to them. "I've fitted in a small table by the window. You can come now."

Camilla was glad for the interruption. Somehow she didn't like to see Marc Butler's eyes filled with the pain of old wounds.

"I can recommend the fish and chips, the salmon, and the oysters," Camilla said.

With an effort Dr. Butler matched her mood. "Good. Then the salmon it shall be." Again he lapsed into boyishness. "Look at that salad bar! Lead me to it!"

In a wave of laughter they filled plates and began their dinner. The past was put back in the past.

Later Camilla would look back and remember — for now it was enough to know she had made a good impression on Dr. Butler. For Jim's sake, she hoped he would stay. She sensed in the man the determination and dedication she felt in Jim himself. If she added in her innermost being, *Not only for Jim's sake,* it wasn't to be thought of or admitted. She had a public relations job to do, and it had gotten off to a flying start.

Chapter 3

Marc Butler was impressed. From kitchen to surgery, from canteen to the shops, Auburn Veterans' Hospital was literally a dream come true. In every instance he could see the careful planning that had made it more than just another hospital. Everything that could be done to make patient care smoother had been included in the plans.

"Dr. Montgomery spent hours with the architects, once Auburn had been approved," Camilla told him. She had shown Marc the entire plant on Saturday. Sunday morning he had gone to chapel with her, impressed by the brief talk the chaplain had given, the heartfelt singing of those who attended.

"I can certainly see that," Marc said. "You really admire Dr. Montgomery, don't you?"

"I love him."

The simple answer plummeted Dr. Butler's heart to the depths. In the short time he had known Camilla Clark, her status in relation to other men had become unbelievably important to him.

His spirits lifted as she added, "Everyone

does." Maybe she didn't mean she loved him personally.

"He is a man to admire," Marc said, then changed the subject. "How about something on the lighter side this afternoon? Sightseeing? Once I get out here working, maybe there won't be time for it."

For a moment Camilla stared at him, her face aglow above the dusty rose outfit she had chosen for church. "You mean — you mean you've already decided to come? Without even seeing Jim — Dr. Montgomery?"

"If he will have me. I've been overwhelmed with the setup here, and with the added attractions."

The color in her face rose. Was that hesitancy in her eyes?

He was rushing ahead too fast. To cover, he waved toward Mt. Rainier, white-capped, beautiful. "Such scenery. So little pollution."

She breathed a little sigh of relief. She wasn't ready for this handsome stranger's compliments, not yet. "How would you like to tour Seattle this afternoon?" She listed several places they could visit in the big city.

"Whoa! One thing at a time! You have to see I eat first. Shall we have dinner in the Space Needle?"

"Not unless you particularly want to. Seattle is full of good places with every kind of food imaginable."

He considered for a moment. "You know what I'd really like? Some more good seafood."

"We can go to Ivar's, then. They're good. Of course, so are lots of other places."

It was a perfect day. Never had Marc Butler felt more at ease with a woman. Camilla didn't chatter every minute. She was restful, matching his mood. They laughed a lot, at simple things. Like the dirty-faced little boy eating an apple on a curb.

Once they passed a couple with two small children out for a walk. A pang went through Marc. He had never really had a family. His father had been too busy making piles of money; his mother, involved in the social whirl of which she was a leader.

"You know, I can't remember even one time we did anything as a family," he said with a wistfulness that brought a lump to Camilla's throat.

How much he'd missed. She thought of her own childhood, rich in love from Dad Montgomery, her own mother, and Jim. They hadn't had much money. Their riches had been of another kind, based on the joy of being together.

"When I have a family, we're going to do things together," she said.

Again, Marc had that odd sinking sensation. "Is it going to be in the near future?" He glanced at her bare third finger, left hand. That didn't always tell all the story.

"No." There was no way Camilla could add to her blunt answer. For a wild moment she wanted to tell him about Jim, how she was committed to helping him, providing a family.

She couldn't do it. He wasn't Jim to Dr. Butler. He was Dr. Montgomery, hospital director and supervisor. She had no right to expose his private life. The moment passed. A squirrel ran down a tree trunk and chattered at them.

"That sassy guy has a lot to say, doesn't he?" Marc picked up a cone and tossed it in the squirrel's direction. He didn't even blink. "He knows he's safe!"

Camilla was glad for the change in the atmosphere. This was no day for too much seriousness.

It was over dinner that Camilla asked, "Marc, how did you ever happen to choose to work with veterans, especially in psychiatry?"

His soup spoon stilled. "I knew someone

who encouraged me." He laughed a little shortly. "No, I won't say encouraged. I was challenged, put to the test. Maybe someday I'll tell you about it." He smiled. "Psychiatry is important today. With all the pressures in today's world, a lot of people need help."

His face became somber. "And who's to say when we won't be plunged into war again? There are trouble spots all over the world." He busied himself with his chowder again. "In the meantime, there are a lot of veterans needing help. Even after all this time, there are still Vietnam soldiers and prisoners of war who have suffered some lasting effects. There are also men and women who have been in the 'peacetime' service. Some of them are coming out with some real problems."

"I know." Unconsciously she sighed. "I see a lot of apathy and anger, and it makes me wonder. If or when we go to war again, God forbid! Sometimes the future looks pretty bleak. Superbombs, wars, threat of wars, pollution — there are so many stormclouds hanging over the world now!"

"Haven't there always been?" He paused, then leaned forward, dinner forgotten. "Look back to the history of this country

48

alone, not to mention the rest of the world. The early settlers nearly starved. Later the pioneers were threatened by Indians. Then World War I. Then the Depression. Then World War II. Camilla, I believe it's out of adversity that strength comes.

"I believe in mankind's ability to pick up the pieces and go on, no matter what. I also believe in a divine spark in every person. Sometimes it's buried so deep there seems to be little chance of it ever being reached or brought into the open. I know this is true, Camilla. If that one spark in me hadn't been reached at the exact time it was, I shudder to think of where I'd be now."

Camilla was caught up in the intensity of his feelings. She felt as if she had been picked up by a whirlwind. So there were still men in the world with what Dad Montgomery would have called "old-fashioned ideals." She'd seen so many who lacked them. It was an experience in itself just talking with Marc Butler.

"Then you feel it takes hardship to bring out people's best?" she asked.

"I do." He smiled across the table. "Maybe you haven't had to face that hardship yet. Some people escape through life without too much tragedy, but such a person is rare."

Her fingers trembled as she remembered Jim. "No, I haven't escaped." She sipped her water, thinking, *What's wrong with you, Cam? In another moment you'll be spilling the story of your life all over him.* Deliberately she pushed down the longing to share her experiences. Just because he was a sympathetic human being was no reason to pour out all her concerns, at least not yet.

She caught his eyes on her and something inside her leaped. After all, he was coming to Auburn to stay. Let the future take care of itself.

Monday and Tuesday were busy days. Dr. Butler wanted to explore every nook and cranny of the hospital more carefully, and did so. Camilla spent time with him, as her schedule permitted, but sometimes she laughingly waved him away.

"Go prowl by yourself. I have to do some paperwork."

It was in these times he began to know some of the other people. He spent most of his time with medical personnel. But he also watched the way the engineering division was run, how the corps of carpenters, painters, electricians, plumbers and machine-shop people worked in harmony.

He even visited with the superintendent of the boiler plant. The more he saw, the more impressed he was. These people were working at jobs they enjoyed. There was pride in their work. They did not work *for* the hospital, but *with* it.

It was an eager Dr. Butler who was ushered into Dr. James Montgomery's office early Thursday morning. His heart was beating rapidly. Suppose Dr. Montgomery changed his mind? Marc had literally fallen in love with the hospital. More than anything he wanted the job.

An early morning ray of sunlight shone through the sparkling window, highlighting the man in the wheelchair. For a moment neither spoke. Each was too busy taking measure of the other.

Marc saw a man several years older than himself, blue eyes keen behind glasses, sandy hair already rumpled a bit. What struck him was not the physical look. There was something about Jim Montgomery as he sat there that defied anyone to feel pity for him. How could a man who looked like that be pitied? He couldn't. The peace he had acquired overrode the suffering he'd gone through. He was a man in control of himself.

Jim Montgomery was not so cool as he appeared. He hadn't realized how tense his muscles were until Dr. Butler had entered.

The newspaper picture had not done him justice, Jim realized. Dr. Marc Butler was tall and straight. His dark hair was brushed smoothly. His dark eyes were watchful. He appeared to be in perfect health. No sign of any kind of dissipation or excess about him.

"What do you think of our hospital?" Jim waved Dr. Butler to a nearby chair, one where he could watch the changing expression on the younger man's face.

Immediately it broke into a smile.

"I love it!" In a lesser man the phrase would have been trite. From Marc Butler it sounded right and had the effect of bringing an answering smile to Jim's lips. The spontaneous response had done more to break the ice between them than anything else could have done.

Marc's face glowed as he reported, "I've peered into every part of your hospital." Neither thought it strange he called it "your" hospital. "I have found nothing that could be improved on. It's perfect."

"Good. Then you'll come and be part of it?"

"If you want me," Marc Butler said.

"I do."

For a moment Dr. Butler's lips trembled. "I think you know how much this means to me —"

He was cut off by Dr. Montgomery's quick motion. "We need you here. It will complete our staff." He held out his hand, the hand he had not offered when the younger man entered his office. "You'll want some time to finish up at your present job, of course." His fingers were strong.

The grip gave Marc Butler strength to compose himself.

"My chief would like me to remain at my present spot a month, if possible," Dr. Butler said.

"Fair enough." Already the emotion was dying. Dr. Montgomery's voice was all business. "In the meantime, we'll see that you get back to the airport for your flight out this evening. I can get one of the motor-vehicle men to take you."

Marc was clearly dismissed. He stood, feeling like a boy but determined to make one request. "I was wondering — that is, Miss Clark was so good about showing me around, I thought if she were free to take me back to the airport . . ." He felt like a floundering fool.

"I see."

Just how much did those keen eyes behind the glasses really see?

A slight smile crossed the stern features. Then Jim said, "That can probably be arranged. I believe the motor-vehicle men are busy enough anyway."

There was nothing in his voice to show his true feelings.

But as Marc left the office he sensed that Dr. Montgomery had been laughing at him. Why? There was no answer, at least then.

Camilla picked Marc up at the chief of staff's home wearing the same red pantsuit she'd worn the night he first saw her. Had it been less than a week? Impossible! Already she'd become part of his mind, appearing at odd moments. He'd always scoffed at the idea of love at first sight, scorning it as impossible, fantasy.

Now his psychiatric background rose to make light of his foolish fancies. He wasn't in love with her, of course not! He refused to listen to the little voice saying, *Then why do you feel as if you'll be leaving part of you behind when you get on that plane?*

They were quiet on the short drive from Auburn to the airport. There were things waiting to be said and yet it was not the time.

It wasn't until they neared the airport that Marc said, "Camilla, I want you to know these last few days have meant a lot to me. I appreciate your playing hostess."

She stared straight ahead, waiting for a

light to change. If her hands inside her driving gloves felt a little sticky, it didn't show.

"I'll be back in a month." He hesitated. She wasn't the kind of person to approach bluntly. He could sense in her a quality that would have made his grandmother call her "a real lady."

But when she finally parked the car and started to get out, he stopped her. Reaching across the seat he clasped her hand. "I'll miss you this month, Camilla."

Before she could speak, he leaned over, put his arm around her, and kissed her sweet red lips. What started as a casual good-bye deepened into a lasting kiss. The touch of her cool lips brought a rush of feeling to Dr. Marc Butler, and his arm tightened about her shoulders.

Camilla had been taken by surprise. She had been kissed before, but not like this. She felt her own lips grow warm under his and hesitated for a moment, heart pounding. Then she pulled back, dark eyes wide.

"Don't come inside, Camilla." Marc had already reached for his suitcase. "Good-bye for a month." Before she could protest, he was gone. When he reached the end of the parking lot, he turned, waved, then stepped through the door of the terminal.

For a long moment Camilla sat in the car, blindly staring at the terminal entrance. No longer could she deny the attraction she'd felt for the dark-haired doctor, even before she'd met him in person. Her lovely skin flushed with color. Was it mere physical attraction? She'd felt that before, but never so keenly.

Her heart denied the charge. It had to be more than that. She thought of the way they had laughed together, talked together seriously, the world of medicine they shared. Was there any reason she shouldn't go all out in letting herself like him? He was a prince among men.

As she backed out and drove through the evening dusk, Camilla Clark remembered a conversation with Jim, from long ago. She had said, "I have a feeling when Mr. Right comes along, nothing on earth will stand in the way. You know how headstrong I am."

It was followed by another remembered conversation, more recent. Jim had said, "Maybe you'll enjoy your public relations duties."

"Sure, I'll probably even fall in love with him," she'd said.

"Never!"

With a dull thud Camilla came back to reality. Why had Jim protested so strongly? He had approved Marc Butler for a top position in his hospital. Then why had he vetoed the idea of Camilla falling in love with the same Marc Butler? Was it that he didn't want to lose her himself? No, he wasn't that selfish. Then what was it?

Did Jim know something about Marc Butler he wasn't telling?

Chapter 4

Camilla's eyes misted as she watched the domiciliary patients being taken to their rooms. She thought: *Imagine, being old and helpless and not having a place to go. I'd rather die young. They're so — so pitiful.* Many of the patients looked forlorn, wounded terribly during past wars. And California had been their home, such as it was. Now they had been sent to this new place in Washington State. In addition to their other problems, they'd have to adjust to their new surroundings.

A few could walk despite their injuries. Camilla impulsively stepped forward to help one of the women. There had only been about six women in this first batch of patients. "Let me."

At first the woman pulled back, but on seeing the white uniform she managed a smile and leaned against Camilla's arm.

"We're glad to have you here." Camilla realized she was chattering a little nervously, but anything was better than seeing the almost stricken look on the woman's face. There were lines of suffering, of pain, etched deep.

"Thank you, dear." When she smiled, the tired eyes lit up. "It's all so new and strange."

Camilla's heart went out to her. "Yes, it is. I can imagine being moved so suddenly, especially following the earthquake, is upsetting. Why, just moving from my room at nurse's training when it was over threw me into a spin for days!"

She was rewarded by another little smile. Encouraged, she confided, "You know Dr. Montgomery is my brother. He's the hospital director." She went on to tell this stranger much of his stormy past. "So you see, he just had to make up his mind to do what he could." She led the woman into her room.

"Montgomery? But your nameplate says Clark."

"Oh, yes. Jim isn't my real brother, but he's looked after me so much I could never have had a better brother." On impulse she added, "Won't you call me Camilla? I won't be in the domiciliary area too much, but if you don't mind, it would be nice if I could come talk with you sometimes when I'm off duty. Since Mom died, I haven't had an older woman to talk with."

The other woman's hand came out, firm and surprisingly strong. "I hope you will come. Oh, I'm Elizabeth Wakefield. I have a weak heart caused by a war injury. But I'm so much more fortunate than the other domiciliary patients. And thank you for what you've done for me today."

Camilla's eyes opened wide with surprise. "What I've done for you? Oh, no, Miss Wakefield. I'm the one to thank you. I don't know when I've been able to open up and tell someone all these things. But somehow you don't seem like a stranger to me."

Elizabeth Wakefield stood. She did not look like the same patient who had come into the hospital a short time before. "I'm Elizabeth to you. I think I'll like it here." Her smile was warm as the young nurse hugged her before leaving.

A few days later provided Jim and Camilla with one of the rare evenings together they treasured so much. They had eaten dinner in the hospital dining room, but raced back to their home for the evening. The weather had turned cold, with icy blue skies and a snap in the air. The fire in the fireplace felt good.

"You'll get a good husband, Camilla."

She looked at him, unable to follow his line of thought. They hadn't been discussing her marital status or anything related to it.

"You know, the fire. Remember how Dad

always said that any woman who could build a good fire would have a smart husband?"

"I'd almost forgotten. From the looks of that fire" — she pointed to the flaming blaze — "I'll marry a genius." There was nothing in the words to bring hot color to her face, but the memory of a dark-eyed man suddenly appeared in the flames.

"Speaking of geniuses, Cam, or would they be geniusii? Anyway, I've been thinking . . ." Was his voice a trifle too casual? "We put Dr. Butler in something of a bad spot. I asked him to come in a month and he said he would. His month will be up just before the Christmas holidays. I wonder if I should write and ask him if he'd like to wait until after Christmas? Or if he does come, it might be nice to invite him to spend Christmas with us. What do you think?"

Marc Butler their guest for the holidays? It took Camilla two tries to answer casually. "That would be nice. He probably will want to spend it with his folks. But if not, it would be lonely here for him."

"Good. I'll write him tomorrow." Then, as an afterthought, Jim said, "Why don't you write a little note to enclose with my letter? After all, you are the lady of the house."

"Fine. I'll do it tonight and you can include it with yours." She had another thought. "Jim, we have a lot of people who will be here for Christmas, the domiciliary residents, a few patients, and so on. Is anything special planned for them?"

"You bet. Volunteers will do a beautiful job. Everyone will receive wrapped gifts, tagged individually. There will be a little tree on all the wards except intensive care. Dinner is going to be as home-cooked and good as we can make it. You know the various churches are coming caroling, and there will be a special Christmas Eve service in the chapel, and regular church services on Christmas Day."

"Good. I'll have to admit I was thinking of Elizabeth, especially. She can get around. But she seems a little lost, at loose ends. Oh, Jim, I meant to ask you. I've been reading that some hospitals with domiciliary patients — who are not completely incapacitated — have programs where the patients can put in a few hours' work in a lot of different ways. They earn a little spending money above and beyond their pensions. Could we have that kind of program? At least Elizabeth could do something when she's up to it."

Jim smiled. "Camilla, Camilla, you always

race ahead, always want to help people. Well, the answer's yes. It's already in the works. As soon as we get it organized, we'll put it in effect. They won't be working on the wards, of course, but anywhere else in the hospital. Maybe in some of the offices or the library. The ones who are able will work two or three hours a day." He laughed outright. "I suppose you already have a spot picked out for your friend Elizabeth?"

"Well, she does have a lot of secretarial experience."

"Good. One of the offices will pick her up. We have plenty of work. It's hard to believe we can have so many patients already."

"That's because you run a good hospital, Dr. Montgomery."

Jim laughed again. "You know, Camilla, you're the best little old morale booster a guy ever had. How'd I get so lucky?" He didn't wait for an answer. "Well, better get to bed." He paused at the door, a wicked glint in his eyes. "Don't forget to write your invitation."

Camilla stared after him. Was he psychic? She had just been waiting for him to leave so she could get to it. For the hundredth time she thought of what a great person he really was. If only he and Alice . . . But there wasn't anything she could do about that.

Or was there? Determination crept into her finely shaped lips and jaw. Reaching for the Seattle telephone directory, she ran her finger down the S column. Shannon, A.C., Shannon, A.L., Shannon, Alice. It was the same address she had visited in what seemed centuries ago. Did she dare call? Why not?

It was wrong to cut off her own friendship with Alice Shannon just because Jim had done so. She dialed.

"Alice? This is Camilla Clark. . . . Yes, really. . . . I know it's been a long time. I was wondering." She closed her eyes, swallowed hard, and took the plunge. "Could we meet for lunch this week?" Long pause. "Yes, that would be fine. I'll see you there, Alice."

She cradled the phone and whirled to see a white-faced Jim. *"Did you say Alice?"* he demanded.

She could feel the color drain from her face. Had she gone too far? She had never seen Jim so angry.

His next words were like bullets searing her flesh. "What are you trying to do? Drum up pity for good old Jim, the cripple?"

"Cripple! How dare you refer to yourself as a cripple?" She glared at him, spurring her own anger on. "You, with this whole hospital to run. You, a cripple? Don't be completely insane!"

Some of the anger drained from his eyes, but his voice was still icy. "Why were you talking to Alice? It was Alice Shannon, wasn't it?"

"I'm meeting her for lunch on Saturday." She closed her eyes against the angry protest in the man's voice. "Just because you dropped her is no reason I have to. I've let years go by and never contacted her. I have every right to choose my own friends, regardless of how you feel about them."

It was in the open, the naked hostility. The unexplored conversation topic had been broached.

Jim's face turned even whiter. "That's right. But I also have a right to choose my friends. Just keep that in mind if you have any little schemes up your sleeve."

"I will." To her horror, Camilla felt hot tears crowding back of her eyes. She hadn't wanted to fight with Jim, to see him look as he now did. How else could it have been managed? She should have called Alice from the hospital itself, then casually announced after their lunch that she had seen her. The next moment her defenses crumbled before the sheer misery in Jim's face. He still cared, terribly. It shone in his eyes.

"I'm sorry, Cam."

In a moment she was on her knees beside him, sobbing into his lap blanket. "I guess I shouldn't have called her. But somehow I just felt like I wanted to see her. We don't have any friends from our old life, and Alice was always so good to me."

Jim's hand lay on the shining dark hair. "It's all right, Cam. You had no way of knowing. You're right. You have to choose your own friends. It's just that I haven't recovered from her letter, and —"

"Letter!" Camilla sat bolt upright. "You had a letter from Alice? When?"

"Two days ago." He fumbled in his pocket. The letter was crushed, as if it had been wadded up and thrown into a wastebasket, only to be retrieved and smoothed out.

His eyes seemed to see beyond the living-room walls. "She wanted to let me know she has met a wonderful man, a doctor. They plan to marry eventually. Right now he's doing some special studies on a grant. He's gone for about a year or so."

Jim hesitated, touching the crumpled pages. "Somehow she heard we still haven't filled the position of director of nurses. She wondered if she could fill the job."

"Alice engaged? Come again?" Camilla's mind was whirling. "She didn't say a word about it when I called."

"Not surprising. She's not the type who would. She put it up to me squarely. She's qualified, she wants to work with the hospital. Would I consider letting her come or would it be too hard for me?"

"How about for her?" Camilla asked.

"For her? She's engaged, remember?" He instantly regretted the bitterness in his voice.

Camilla was sharp about noticing things. To his relief she didn't seem to catch it this time.

"What are you going to do?" she asked.

"I don't know." His frank admission seemed to clear the air. "She's the best all-round nurse I know. We need her, the hospital needs her. I'm just not sure if I can stand having her see me like this day in, day out."

His despair gripped Camilla's throat. Will power triumphed over pity in her little laugh. "It's barely possible the director of nurses might be a little too busy to be seeing the hospital director day after day, you know."

Jim straightened. "You're right at that. At first I thought the whole idea was preposterous. Then I thought of how much she could mean in that position. The director of nurses has a tremendous responsibility. She has to know, encourage, and look out for every nurse in this hospital. Frankly, that's why I've held off hiring someone. You know the woman who was coming discovered her husband has cancer. She withdrew her application. I've been stumped to find someone qualified."

"Why don't you wait until after Saturday? Maybe I can find out more when I see her."

"I'd appreciate that." His fingers drummed on the wheelchair arm. "If I really thought she was happy in her engagement to this Dr. Jones, I could probably accept her application. All I ever wanted was her happiness."

"And your own?"

"I'm not unhappy, Cam. I had to release dreams years ago. Once I did, I found a certain peace, even contentment. I have my job, and you." His smile was unexpectedly sweet. "What more could any man ask?"

Long after Camilla had gone to bed that night, she thought of the situation. What would come of the whole thing? Dr. Jones, Alice's fiance. What kind of man was he? Had he replaced Jim in her heart, or made a new place of his own?

There were many kinds of love. Perhaps Alice had found a different kind than the first love for Jim. She was a woman now, in her thirties. It wasn't right for her to spend her life alone. Yet did she remember the times when she and Jim had dreamed together?

Camilla had her answer on Saturday. The Alice Shannon who rose to meet her was not the person she had known. She was much quieter, as if life had subdued her. At first things were awkward, and Camilla was glad they were in a fairly crowded restaurant.

But when they finished eating, Alice said, "Please come home with me."

Camilla could not refuse.

The apartment was the same — warm and welcoming. So was Alice. On entering her own home she seemed to shed the slightly aloof manner of the restaurant. Her first words took Camilla completely by surprise.

"You will find it hard to believe, but if you hadn't called me, I was going to call you."

Camilla gasped.

"It's true. Camilla, I want you to do something for me. I want you to influence Jim to give me the director of nurses job."

Camilla couldn't believe her ears. Alice had always been direct, but she certainly hadn't expected this!

"Ever since the day Jim sent me away, I've wanted to do something for him. This will be my last chance. He wouldn't let me share his personal life, although his being in a wheelchair would never have stopped me. It was Jim I loved, not the fact he could walk. He chose to end that love. Now there's a chance to help him professionally." She caught Camilla's look of surprise. "Oh, yes, I have kept informed on Jim all these years."

Alice suddenly dropped her crisp way of speaking and leaned forward. "Camilla, Dr. Jones will be through with his studies in a year or so. In the meantime, I'd like to work at the Auburn hospital."

Camilla couldn't hold back the question. "Will you be able to see Jim day after day without remembering?"

"Without remembering! Do you think a day has passed since the accident that I haven't remembered?" Her passionate tone silenced Camilla. It was from the heart.

In spite of her compassion, Camilla's mind registered the thought, *Will I ever feel like that about anyone?*

"Call it quixotic, call it a gift of love, I don't care. But, Camilla, I want this job more than I've ever wanted anything else in the world — except one thing."

And that thing was Jim. Camilla knew it without being told.

"Alice, I'll do everything in my power to

get you the job." Her voice broke. "Does Dr. Jones know about Jim?"

"Yes."

The room hung in the silence until Camilla stood. "I have to get back. Jim will inform you officially, but I think you'll hear from him soon. He still has his own dragons to fight at times, but they aren't so big anymore."

"I'll be waiting."

As Camilla rode the bus back to Auburn, Alice's words haunted her. *I'll be waiting.* Hadn't Alice's entire life been one of waiting? First for Jim to get through school. Then Vietnam. Then the long agonizing nights and days after the accident, followed by years of wondering. Had she thought Jim would relent, call her back? Had she answered the phone wondering if it could be him? Now she was waiting for Dr. Jones to finish his studies — and for Jim's answer.

"Well, how is Alice?" Jim tried to keep his voice light.

"She seems to have found peace and contentment."

"And happiness?"

"I don't know." Camilla faced him. "She wants this job more than anything in life." She paused. "I think you should hire her."

71

She couldn't add, *Alice wants it more than anything — except one.*

"Did she mention Dr. Jones?"

"Only casually. He has his special studies to finish. Then they'll be married."

"I see."

She could see Jim mulling it over in his mind.

Camilla couldn't hold it back. "Jim, give her this gift. This gift of love." She could see his look of surprise. "Somehow it means everything to her. Let her come."

"All right." He pushed back from the table, leaving the rest of the dinner Camilla had prepared so carefully untouched on his plate.

She could hear him in his room, dictating into his tape recorder. The next day his secretary would transcribe the letter asking Alice Shannon to come and interview for the position of director of nurses.

But even Camilla, straining her ears in the kitchen to listen, could not know how Dr. Jim Montgomery dropped his head in his hands when that letter had been dictated, the letter to bring Alice back into his life.

Chapter 5

It had been a long shift for Marc Butler. He had taken over a night shift as a favor to a fellow doctor. Now he was glad it was nearly over. One more hour and he'd be free.

The patients were finally all asleep. Marc glanced out the window. Full moon. He smiled, a little grimly.

Many people laughed at the idea of a full moon having any significance. He knew better. He'd worked with enough mental patients to note the increased activity during the full moon. He'd also checked out police statistics. They confirmed there was more violent crime during the full moon than at other times. Why? No one knew that. It was true, however.

It had taken a long time for his patients to settle down. Thank God for the use of tranquilizers. They had done more for the psychiatric patient than anything in years, Marc believed. He thought of earlier days, how psychotic patients were treated with restraints. With the use of drugs had come a whole new way of life in working with the mentally disturbed.

Marc sighed. In spite of the so-called "wonder drugs" there was still no complete answer. Why did two men who faced the approximate same situation react so differently? One would be able to meet the problems and pick up the pieces and go on. The other would grow hostile, or retreat into the private self sometimes beyond even trained psychiatric help.

The day would come when new breakthroughs would aid those who probed into the patient's brain.

He sat down at the desk, feet on the waste can. It would only be a few days until he would be through here. With a wrench he realized how much he'd miss this place, and yet — his heart beat a little faster, thinking of Auburn Veterans' Hospital. There would be plenty of work for him there among the veterans of World War I, World War II, the Korean War, Vietnam.

Vietnam. For the first time in years Marc forced himself to remember. He glossed over the actual fighting, thought of the crashing plane, the capture of the group of men. It had been horrible. Every story of prisoner-of-war camps was true. The stench. The lack of food. The deliberate playing on the emotion of men, trying to break their spirit.

How had any of them kept their sanity? There had been those who "cooperated" with their captors, who had even played turncoat and had been released. But released to what? To a world pointing the finger at them as cowards?

Marc Butler had hated those who turned and denied their own country. Yet he had pitied them. He had never known how much it would take to break him. How could he judge who was weak? How much torture could anyone take? How had anyone ever come home at all from that hell on earth?

The rigidity left his frame and a warm glow started inside. The reason they had come home had been because of their commanding officer. Dirty, unshaven, hungry as the rest, he had refused to let his men despair.

"Who knows?" Jim Montgomery had said. "Maybe we'll be out tomorrow. We'll go home and eat steak and mashed potatoes and apple pie, and . . ."

Marc's eyes glistened as he remembered. The sheer dynamic quality of that C.O. had kept some of his men alive.

Then they came home. There was hospitalization. Tests, hundreds of them, it seemed. But at last they were free, the captain and his men. Free to take up life as it had been?

No. They would never be able to do that again. Instead they would have to painstakingly carve new futures.

But before they did, they were to have a farewell party.

Dr. Butler's hands clenched. Perspiration formed on his forehead. Usually at this point in his thoughts he would resolutely wipe out the rest. Not this time. Here in the early morning hours of a quiet ward, just before getting ready to go to another position, was the time to face it, then put it away forever. But could such a thing be put away forever?

Marc Butler saw the boy he had been lift high the glass and say, "To the future!" Then: "Captain, to you!" It was the only way he knew to pay tribute without turning maudlin.

Down the corridor of years came the whisper, "Haven't you had about enough?"

There was agony in Dr. Butler's face as he remembered his answer. "No, sir!" Another drink, then another, until he said, "Here's to everybody!" There had been a mighty swing of his arm. A heavy glass knocked a candle toward the sheer curtains. Flames leaped. The man responsible stood staring at them, his mind clouded by too many drinks.

The rest of the nightmare had been mercifully obliterated. Marc could vaguely remember men rushing past, the captain herding them outside. He remembered knowing he must put out the fire. He started toward the blaze, trying to clear his mind, to walk steadily. It was impossible. Then something struck him. There was a period of soft blackness.

When he awoke, it was in a hospital, bandaged, with a headache to end all headaches.

"What happened?" Marc had asked.

"No talking now." The crispness of the nurse matched her white cap and uniform.

Strange, he didn't even care. He sank back to sleep again, barely aware of the faint prick of a needle in his arm.

The next time he woke, his head was clear. He remembered, at least partially. "How did I get out?"

What was there in his question to make the nurse look at him so coldly before answering? After a long pause, she said, "Captain Montgomery pulled you out."

"Captain? No kidding!" He laughed a bit foolishly. "Guess I wasn't in too hot a shape."

"No, you weren't." Again that same hint of censure. Why did this nurse dislike him? He'd never even seen her before. Then he found out. She faced him squarely. "Captain Montgomery was hurt getting you out."

"Hurt? The captain?" Marc threw back the sheet. "I have to go see him."

"You can't. He can't see anyone for a while." The nurse's face was grave as she pushed him back into bed.

Marc's face felt frozen, his mouth dry. "He wasn't hurt — hurt bad, was he?"

"I'm afraid so. They don't think he'll ever walk again." The look on her patient's face softened the nurse's voice, but his parchment skin alarmed her. "There's nothing you can do, now at least. Stay in bed."

He turned from her, refusing to look at her again. "It was my fault."

Compassion filled her eyes. At first she had been enraged that a man like Captain Montgomery would be crippled because of the stupid, drunken act of one of his men.

Now she touched his arm. "He chose to go back, you know. He wouldn't leave one of his men."

There was no answer to show he had heard. With a sigh, she placed the call cord near his hand. "If you need anything, ring."

He barely heard the door shut. Waves of nausea swept through him. Everything that had been done to him in Vietnam was as nothing compared to what he went through that night. His captain. The man he admired more than anyone on earth. From the moment he had met Jim Montgomery, Marc had idolized him. He was everything Marc wished his own father could be — and wasn't. He was the kind of man Marc would like to be — and wasn't. He was someone to rely on, to almost worship. *And now he was lying a helpless cripple because of Marc.*

So during the days he should have been recuperating, Marc Butler was facing the biggest fight of his life. Wouldn't it be better if he just jumped off a bridge when he got out of the hospital? His own worthless life continually flashed off and on, reminding him of the contrast between his own life and that of Jim Montgomery's. The only thing Marc had ever really been proud of doing was going to Vietnam, and look how that had ended!

He fought his battle, responding woodenly to those around him. Until the night came when he could stand it no longer. He had to see the captain. Maybe they were wrong. Maybe he wasn't really hurt so badly.

He had learned to time the nurses' rounds. All was still as Marc slipped from the bed, still shaky from his own burns. He crept down the hall, avoiding linen closets where nurses might be. Slowly he made his way to a certain room. He had listened avidly to conversations not meant for his ears and discovered where Jim Montgomery was. The door creaked a bit, but there was no other sound. Like a wraith from the past, Marc got inside, turned toward the bed.

"What are you doing in here?" Jim Montgomery had demanded.

Strange how the years hadn't lessened the challenge in that voice, the exact words of a commanding officer wanting to know why one of his men was in his hospital room late at night. Just as faithfully, his memory produced the answer. "I had to come, sir. Captain Montgomery, can you ever forgive me?"

Dr. Butler was recalled from the past by one of the nurses, who said, "Patient in room 3 is disturbed. Can you see him?"

Instantly he was all doctor. All it took was listening to the man's rambling. He needed someone to hear what he had to say.

When Marc returned to his solitary post, he thought to himself, Isn't that what the world's all about? Everyone needs people to hear what they say, and no one has time to listen.

He sank back in his chair, determined to finish his self-induced trip to the past. Captain Montgomery had listened. He had heard more than the cry of a repentant man. He had heard the spirit inside struggling to get out. He had spoken to that spirit, asking if Marc would fulfill his own dream of life, in his place.

In all the years following, Marc had never wavered. Deep inside he knew he could never fill Captain Montgomery's shoes. He wasn't that big a man. He knew of no other man on earth who would do what Jim Montgomery had done, not only challenge, but follow up the progress. Marc hadn't known until he received the letter of invitation to visit Auburn Veterans' Hospital how intensely Jim had followed up. He had evidently kept a pretty close watch on the career of the man who would make his own dream come true.

I will see he never regrets it. Even as he had pledged himself years before to follow that dream, Marc renewed his pledge. He would do everything in his power to become the kind of doctor Jim wanted.

Auburn Veterans' Hospital. Created by a man in a wheelchair. Marc had kept quiet track of his former C.O. during the busy years. He had known of the fight he was making, both personally and professionally. He had literally wept tears of joy when he heard Dr. James Montgomery was to be hospital director of the new veterans' hospital.

What did it matter to Dr. Montgomery that he was hampered by a wheelchair? He had transcended that wheelchair in a million ways. The last and perhaps most significant was the deliberate seeking out of the man who had put him there.

A rosy, glowing streak of dawn heralded the end of Marc's shift. It also heralded the beginning of a new day. After the quiet, soul-searching he had done, Marc felt ready for it. He was on top of the world. Behind lay years of making up for his indolent, careless youth. Ahead lay Auburn Veterans' Hospital.

The image of a glowing, dark-haired nurse slipped into Marc's mind. Camilla Clark. A lovely name for a lovely person. Even in the short days he had spent in her company he'd fallen hard. All the college-day romances were eclipsed by the feeling that had begun to develop. Could she ever care for him? She must. When he had given in to impulse and kissed her good-bye, her lips had responded. He had felt it in the little tremble.

The future lay ahead, and with it Camilla. But first he must get to know her, let her know him. It was unbelievable that she hadn't been snatched up before now. She was such a rare person. Basically quiet, yet she could radiate warmth. What if she already cared for someone?

"She can't! She's mine!" He hadn't realized how loud he had spoken until an approaching nurse stopped and stared. Dr. Butler was certainly vehement about something!

"Sorry," he laughed at her. "I talk to myself sometimes." He swung out the door, his shift ended, leaving a nurse watching him and wondering why he looked as if he'd just been given the whole Christmas tree.

It was late afternoon before Marc awakened. It was also the best sleep he'd had in months. The world looked good. A brisk shower, a combination breakfast/lunch put him on top of things again.

Later he would remember how at that moment he'd felt nothing on earth could touch him, tear him down. He would remember with scorn for the mortal being he was. He would remember rereading the words that would change his whole life.

Office of Hospital Director, Auburn Veterans' Hospital, Auburn, Washington. Must be some last-minute details from Dr. Montgomery.

Funny, Marc thought they'd settled everything. Dr. Montgomery had assured him
there would be quarters ready. Why was he
writing to him now? He opened the single
page. It was typed, to the point.

Dear Dr. Butler,
I am wondering if you would like to
spend the Christmas holidays with us.
When we set it up for you to come in a
month, neither of us was thinking that
would be just before Christmas. You'd
be more than welcome.
If you have family obligations, of
course we'll understand. If not, we will
look for you on December 23rd, as origi-
nally planned. Your tour of duty doesn't
actually start until the 26th. Our home is
open to you if you care to come.

Sincerely,
James Montgomery, M.D.

A warm wave of surprise swept through
Marc. Was there ever such a man as Jim
Montgomery? If he had idolized the man
before, this new evidence of his concern and
caring changed it to almost worship. A little
frown crossed Marc's face. Dr. Montgomery had used the plural:

"spend the Christmas holidays with us."

Was Dr. Montgomery married? Marc didn't think so. Perhaps he had a mother or father living with him. Strange, nothing had been mentioned about it. Why had he said "us"?

As Marc replaced the letter in the envelope, a smaller note dropped out. He hadn't seen it before. He glanced at the signature before reading. Camilla Clark. He could feel color rush to his face.

Dear Marc,

Just a note to drop in with Jim's. We hope you will be able to spend the holidays with us. We already have snow and it looks as if it will stick. Hope you can come.

Your new friend,
Camilla Clark

Chapter 6

Marc stared at the note. How odd that there would be an enclosure from Camilla in Dr. Montgomery's invitation. Even stranger was the fact she had referred to his coming, using the word "us." A faint premonition chilled him. Was there something between Dr. Montgomery and Camilla? No. He remembered when she'd said simply, "I love him," she had also added, "Everyone does."

His frown smoothed out as he reread the two invitations. Evidently Dr. Montgomery had seen how impressed he'd been with Camilla Clark and asked her to reiterate the invitation.

Marc had almost forgotten how V.A. hospital employees always looked on the hospital as a giant extended family. It was automatic for them to speak of "us," in referring to the hospital itself.

With a sigh of relief he reached for a pen. No, on second thought, he'd send a telegram. It would give them a little extra time in case it was needed for preparations.

Christmas with Camilla! A new job, new challenges, a new life. The rosy dawn he had seen earlier that morning was beckoning.

"He's coming!" Camilla waved the yellow telegram. "He'll be here the 23rd just as you asked."

Jim's eyes were mischievous. "I suppose you'll want a hospital guard to go meet him?"

"Oh, I can go." Her tone was casual, betrayed by the flags of color on her face. "I have everything done. I might as well pick him up. It will seem a little friendlier."

"How come he's flying? Doesn't he have a car?"

"He mentioned once when he was here his car was old. He thought he'd sell it. Maybe he shipped everything ahead and decided to buy a new one here rather than have to mess with license-plate changing, different states and all."

There was a spirit of Christmas throughout the hospital these days. On the wards where there were no critical patients, soft Christmas music was piped in. There were decorations and visiting carolers, just as Jim had said.

One evening the off-duty nurses gathered together, took tall, lighted white candles, and caroled through the halls. Camilla carried her candle with pride, remembering the candlelight service in which she had been capped. Her eyes stung. What a beautiful world! Had anyone ever been any luckier than she was at this particular moment?

When the carolers reached the domiciliary area, Elizabeth Wakefield was one of the first to step out and listen. True to her promise, Camilla had spent some off-duty time with her. Elizabeth was more at home now. For the domiciliary patients who weren't too incapacitated, the new "work if desired" program would go into effect after the holidays.

"I can't stand feeling useless," Elizabeth had confided. "And I can move about most of the time. So it will be good to work a few hours a day." She was going to do clerical work in engineering, when her condition permitted. They were always busy there; the two secretaries carried a big load. Elizabeth would be invaluable in helping file orders, xeroxing, and simple typing.

Then all at once it was the 23rd. On her desk calendar Camilla had circled the date in red, feeling foolish when she did so. Oh, well, no one would ever see it. If she wanted to act like a silly schoolgirl with a crush, it wasn't anyone else's business. Besides, she'd been too busy to participate in such things as a teenager. While she'd dated a number of men since then, none of them had stirred her as deeply as Marc Butler had done with his farewell kiss.

She put on the red pantsuit. The collar of her crisp white blouse spread over the red jacket, making a perfect background for two red rosebuds. A dozen of them and been delivered that afternoon, with a card saying simply, *Merry Christmas, Marc.*

Fortunately Jim hadn't been home to see her face. By the time he arrived, she could tell him casually that Marc Butler had sent the roses, and how thoughtful his hostess gift was.

I'm totally happy, Camilla thought. The looking-glass girl confirmed her thought. She positively radiated good health and happiness. "It's not only for me," she told the image.

It wasn't. Jim had asked a few days before, "Why don't we ask Alice Shannon for dinner on Christmas Day? She came in today and I interviewed her for the director of nurses position. She'll be coming permanently after the first of the year. In the meantime, her fiance can't get home for the holidays and she'll be alone. I just thought it might be nice if we asked her."

Not by even the slightest movement did Camilla betray her surprise. It was quite a step, his wanting Alice to come. Was it some kind of test he was giving himself?

As if in answer to her unspoken question, Jim commented, "After all, there's no reason for us not to be friends. The past is over. She has Dr. Jones and I have my work. There's no reason we can't be friends." There was nothing in his voice to show the decision had come only after hours of soul-searching, of telling himself that same thing, over and over.

Camilla didn't question him. "Fine. You know I'm taking a few days off. I haven't been able to cook a big holiday dinner in years. I can hardly wait!"

Alice had accepted immediately. "Good! I was wondering how to spend my day."

The hands on the clock seemed to be moving backward, but at last it was time to go to the airport. Fortunately the light snow of the afternoon had stopped. Camilla didn't have any trouble getting to the airport. This time she was ahead of Marc. When he stepped into view, her heart gave a most ridiculous jump. She knew her face had a high color.

"Merry Christmas, Camilla!" He caught her hands in his own. More than anything he wanted to kiss the tempting red lips now smiling in welcome, crush this dark-haired girl in his arms, and keep her there forever.

Repression sent a stain of dark color to his own face. Even in this day of careless embraces, he could sense Camilla wouldn't welcome such a scene, especially in public. Kissing her good-bye had been one thing. Snatching her up as if he were a caveman ready to carry her off by the hair would be something else. He chuckled at his mental image. Boy, what would she think if she could know what he was thinking? There was something good to be said for primitive days, after all!

The drive home seemed all too short. They had just arrived when it did start snowing in earnest. White flakes lit on their hair, standing like stars against darkness. Hand in hand, they ran laughing to the house as children would do.

"We can go sledding tomorrow," she said.

"What, no snowmen?" Marc asked.

Her eyes opened wide. "Snowmen? I haven't built one since I was a child."

"Neither have I."

This time she laughed outright and pushed open the door of the hospital director's home, saying, "Welcome to Auburn Veterans' Hospital, Dr. Butler!" An imp lurked in her dark eyes, but before Marc could respond, Dr. Montgomery appeared in the doorway .

"Come in, come in, Dr. Butler!" Jim held out a strong hand. "We're glad to have you for the holidays."

Again the use of the word "we." Marc looked around. No one else in sight. Jim Montgomery must have meant on behalf of himself, the hospital, and Camilla.

"What a charming home!"

It was. Simple, all one story, it was furnished tastefully rather than expensively. There were lots of browns and oranges and yellows.

The living-room fireplace held a roaring fire, casting grotesque shadows on sturdy, livable furniture. A hall ran the length of the house with bedrooms and baths branching off on each side. A sparkling kitchen and small dining room were at the back of the house.

"We like it." Dr. Montgomery smiled. "Hang your coat in the closet. Camilla, will you show Dr. Butler his room?"

"I'd like to be called Marc while off duty."

Jim Montgomery smiled. "Fine. I don't hold with formality except in the hospital itself. It's better there for our staff to use Dr. and Nurse or Miss. Away from duty I like first names."

Marc marveled at the ease with which Camilla welcomed him to Dr. Montgomery's home. She seemed perfectly at home. A light supper was served on trays. Evidently she had prepared it earlier. He wondered where she'd found the time. But the welcome of the two overrode any qualms.

"I don't know when I've felt so excited over the prospect of a new job," he told them. He had helped Camilla with the dishes and all of them had gravitated toward the fireplace. "At the risk of boring you with shoptalk, can you give me a little more information as to exactly what you'd like to see in the psychiatric department?"

Jim's eyes glowed. "Shoptalk is what we do the most of!" He paused. Camilla could see the intensity of his blue eyes boring into Marc Butler's.

"I'd like to see the day when any mental patient who comes in here can be restored to wholeness," Jim continued. "At present, we fail with some. Some have to be transferred to more secure surroundings. We have an excellent staff of highly trained personnel. You'll be in charge of the entire psychiatric program for the hospital. In addition to the regular psychiatric ward, we have those on other wards who'll need your help. Medical and surgical wards, drug and alcohol programs — they'll all call for you and your staff.

"I want any man or woman in this hospital who needs someone to listen to him to be able to find that someone. Not when he or she can be scheduled, but when someone is needed! So many times when a patient needs a listening ear, there's no one available. By the time an appointment is set up, the problem has either grown so big it's hard to handle, or it's been locked back up inside.

"We get a lot of patients. We do a lot of counseling. I visualize the day when the caring of our staff can get through to all the poor devils who have lost control of their lives."

In the fireplace, a stick broke, showering sparks, creating a diversion. But Dr. Jim Montgomery wasn't through.

"There comes a time in the life of every person, I am convinced, when that person could go either way. I have heard some of my colleagues sneer at those who break down mentally, those same doctors who would jump to help someone with a broken leg or a ruptured appendix. I have even heard a few boast that nothing could break their minds. I have nothing but contempt for their ignorance. Every person stands at many crossroads. If too many things pile up, the strongest character is going to break." His hands gripped the arms of his wheelchair.

"I went through my own crisis," he went on. "Only by the grace of God did I get through it. I take no credit. I was at a point where my mind could have gone either way, I think. I was one of the fortunate ones. It took a long time, but I pulled through. Others will face different crises. They may include the death of loved ones, other tragedies, a hundred different pressures. When those pressures mount too much, there will be an explosion, a turning point.

"I want to see our hospital prevent those explosions. Many cannot live through them, and come out on top — as I did."

Camilla swallowed hard, glad for the dimness of the lighting and the flames in the fireplace. Involuntarily her eyes sought Marc's, but he wasn't looking at her. He was staring at Jim, his gaze almost riveted.

When Marc spoke, his voice was hoarse. "Then you believe that after that turning point, that tragedy, nothing will ever be the same?" There was a curious intensity, a waiting for an answer that would come.

"I do. When a man has faced the worst in life, he will either sink under it, or become something far better. He will not be the same."

The ensuing stillness was broken as Marc

Butler got to his feet, a set look on his face. "Dr. Montgomery — Jim — I'll do everything in my power to fulfill your dream." He shook hands with Jim.

As the two hands clasped, Camilla had the curious feeling time had fled to the past. Why should this scene remind her of something, something she couldn't put her finger on? Impatiently she brushed whatever it was from her mind. The room was tense, filled with drama from Marc's acceptance of what Jim had said.

"Let's have some light in here," she said deliberately breaking the spell. "Jim, didn't you say there was a special Christmas program you wanted to watch?"

Jim drew in a ragged breath. The scene they had played had drained him. He caught himself before blurting out something best left unsaid, but smiled at Camilla and Marc. "Yes, there's a telecast of *The Messiah*. I think I'll watch it from my room." He turned to Marc. "You'll never know how glad I am you're here."

With a smile and wave of his hand, Jim rolled down the hall to his own room, leaving the strange impression that a parade had gone by, flags waving, marching men striding with heads held high.

"He's quite a guy," Marc said.

"Yes, he is." Camilla smiled. "I'm so glad you've come. He has never opened up to me like that before. It's been rough for him, you know. It was good for him to get it out of his system."

"Are you only glad I've come on his account, Camilla?"

She pretended to misread his meaning. "Of course not. You're just what the hospital needs. Jim's told me that you have a strong background, excellent credentials." She didn't add she had actually read those credentials. "You will be a valuable asset here."

Marc wisely dropped the subject. She was not one to commit herself on short notice. If there was a biding-my-time glint in his eyes, he carefully hid it. Suddenly he felt he needed to get away from the emotion-charged room. "Camilla, let's go for a walk."

"A walk?" She stared at him. "Do you know it's snowing, eleven o'clock at night?"

"So live dangerously. I'd like to see the hospital in its blanket of snow."

She relented. "All right." She pulled her heavy coat and boots from the closet, handing him his overcoat. "It's cold, but not too cold."

That walk was one that neither of them would ever forget. It seemed the most natural thing in the world to be walking together, gloved hands linked. Not in a romantic sense, but in comradeship.

The snow was new, fresh, covering all the familiar landmarks, giving the hospital softened outlines. Trees were hung with ermine toppings, the boughs bent from the growing weight. Big flakes clung to shrubs. The whole world was silenced by a white hush.

"It's beautiful. Southern California was never like this," Marc said.

"I couldn't live where I couldn't see the seasons change. Tomorrow the snow will probably be all dirty, even a headache to drivers. But when it first comes, it seems to cover the world, hide some of its troubles."

"You're a philosopher, Camilla."

"No. I just like to see the world like this sometimes. It makes up for so much of the ugly in life. I believe the beauty is always there. We can't catch it all the time. When we do, it is even more beautiful because of the contrast."

"I'm glad I could share this moment with you," he said.

"Me, too." The snow was no whiter than the smile she gave him. "But we'd better get back. It's getting late."

Glowing lights from homes decorated for Christmas marked their way. In those homes where people were still up, glimpses of Christmas trees could be seen through windows with curtains still open. When had Marc seen Christmas decorations such as these?

In his own home they had been oddly shaped, almost ugly silver or gold, gaudy and expensive, bearing little relation to Christmas. Here they seemed homier. Some were elaborate, some simple, yet all spoke of pride and love and happiness — all the things Christmas stood for.

"Thank you for tonight, Camilla." They had reached Dr. Montgomery's home. "Don't take your outdoor things off. Do you live close? Can't I drive you home? I wouldn't mind walking back."

Camilla stared at him. "Drive me home? I am home. I live here." She was unprepared for the look that came into Marc's eyes. What was it? Disappointment, scorn, dislike? Or a combination? Whatever it was caused her to add, "Didn't you know?"

Marc looked at her steadily. "No. No, I didn't know." He stepped into the hall behind her, shed his snowy coat, and hung it in the closet. His voice was icy, his eyes burning as he turned back to her. "Thank you for wearing my roses, Miss Clark. Good night."

The next moment he was gone, down the long hall to his room, leaving Camilla staring after him, dripping melted snowflakes on the entryway floor.

Chapter 7

For a holiday that was supposed to be merry, this Christmas failed the test. Camilla stood by her window. Christmas Day was nearly over. Tomorrow they would be back in the workaday world.

She bit her lip. Why had she thought it would be so great to have Marc Butler with them? It had been nothing short of a disaster. For a moment she thought of the night he had arrived, the laughing happy time they'd had, the long walk in the snow.

The picture was brushed out by his icy tone in the hall: "No. No, I didn't know. . . . Thank you for wearing my roses, Miss Clark."

Miss Clark. When he had called her Camilla from the moment they first met! Her face burned in remembrance. It burned even more hotly as she thought of their strange interview the next morning. She had been up early after not having slept well. All night long his accusing dark eyes had watched her from the corners of her room. What must he think? He evidently didn't know Jim was her brother.

Of course! That explained his shock at her statement that she lived there. With a measure of peace, she curled up and slept a few hours. But at the first crack of dawn she was up. As soon as he came into the living room, she would tell him the whole story.

Curled up in a warm, quilted housecoat Camilla waited. She had switched on the lights on the Christmas tree and built up the fire. Something of the room's quietness settled her down. In a few moments Marc would come in and things could be straightened out between them.

It hadn't worked out that way. She had no way of knowing the miserable night Marc Butler had put in. He had run the gamut of emotions. Suspicion: was this Jim Montgomery's revenge? His anger burned as he thought of that little smile in Dr. Montgomery's office when he'd asked if Camilla could drive him to the airport. He had thought nothing of it at the time. Now he wondered. Had it been satisfaction, knowing what lay ahead?

He remembered his first stirring of alarm when the invitations had come, and the use of the words "we" and "us." How ready he had been to convince himself it was the way of the hospital! Jim Montgomery's face floated in his mind. There was no malice in it, no hatred. But what other explanation could there be?

Long after the room had grown cold, even after the snow outside stopped, Marc wrestled with the problem. There had to be an explanation. Was Camilla a housekeeper? No, she couldn't be. Her nursing duties wouldn't leave time for that.

It must have been after four when the explanation came to him. *Camilla was Jim Montgomery's wife.* It was the only logical thing to believe. He thought of her clear dark eyes, her sweetness. It must be true. He tried to tell himself he didn't care. It was no use. And yet, if Camilla were really Camilla Montgomery, why did she go by the name of "Miss Clark"?

Surely they must know the hospital would see through their little ruse. Torn by his own growing love for her, he tried to reason. It was impossible. Marc remembered the way her lips had responded when he kissed her good-bye on his initial visit to Auburn.

Could she have done that if she were another man's wife? *No!* Another woman, perhaps. Not Camilla. In spite of the evidence piling up against her, he would stake his life on her honor, her loyalty.

When the clock struck six, Marc could stand it no longer. Slipping into the adjoining bathroom, he shaved, showered, and dressed. When Camilla got up, he would ask her pointblank if she was married to Jim. He had a right to know that much.

When Marc stepped into the living room, he caught his breath. The rich glowing red of Camilla's robe highlighted her dark hair. Unshed tears sparkled in her eyes. There were faint shadows under their brilliance. She evidently hadn't slept well.

"Good morning." He kept his voice low, casual. Peering out the window, he commented, "Looks as if the snow has stopped."

His easy greeting gave Camilla confidence. She left the chair by the fireplace and came to the window to stand by him. "Marc." In spite of herself, her voice trembled. "About last night —"

Evidently there was to be no conventional smoothing over between them, no courteous ignoring of what had happened. He was glad. He swung toward her, gripping her forearms with fingers of steel. She cringed inwardly. There would be bruises tomorrow.

His voice was hoarse. "Camilla, tell me just one thing. Are you Jim Montgomery's wife?"

"Wife!" Color sped to her hairline. She laughed nervously, remembering when she had proposed just such a thing to Jim. "Of course not. He wouldn't. . . . I asked . . ." She knew her words were garbled but couldn't seem to get herself collected.

"I see." He dropped her arms, a mocking smile on his face.

It was too much for her. Fury burned up the tears just back of her eyelids. Her voice was low but perfectly clear as she told him, "You don't see anything! You don't know anything about Jim or about me! You stand there condemning me because I live here. You have no right to judge appearances without knowing all the circumstances."

His cynical laugh spurred her on.

"This is my home. I have every right to be here. Jim Montgomery is my —"

"Please, Miss Clark." His raised hand stilled her protests. "If you don't mind, I really find this whole conversation rather boring. Now if you'll excuse me, I think I'll walk over to the hospital for breakfast, look around a bit. I'll be back later today."

Camilla was left staring at a closed door. If she had been the kind to let loose her emotions, she would have stamped and screamed in rage. For the first time in her life she wanted to throw things, to force that arrogant man to listen.

The feeling carried her through the holidays. She hated him. The man who was to do great things for her brother's hospital. She hated him more than any other person she had ever known except one, and that was the one who'd put Jim in a wheelchair.

Christmas Eve came and went. Camilla and Marc played their parts to the hilt. Even Jim Montgomery didn't suspect how things were between them. An unspoken truce for the holidays, a ceasing of direct fire, but no amnesty given. If they spent sleepless hours at night, no one would know.

Alice Shannon appeared early Christmas morning. For a moment Jim caught his breath. She hadn't changed. The same soft brown hair and eyes. The same look of gentle strength.

"Hello, Jim. It's been a long time."

"Too long." He took her hand and smiled at her. "So you're going to accept our offer."

If Alice Shannon took a quick breath, he did not see it. All he saw was the woman he had loved so many years ago. Of course, he could see changes now. There was a little gray in the brown hair. A few wrinkles were visible, even though she was still young.

Something inside Jim Montgomery that had been a frozen knot began to loosen. He turned toward the Christmas tree, frantically blinking mist from his eyes. Good grief, he hadn't come unglued when he'd interviewed her. What was wrong with him now?

Alice sensed his discomfort. "You know, my Dr. Jones would have loved to join us. He called this morning, wished everyone Merry Christmas."

It was just the touch needed to restore Dr. Montgomery's normalcy. Dr. Jones, the fiance. Oh, yes. Instantly Jim pulled himself together again and he was able to respond, a bit more heartily than necessary, "Say, if he's all that good, maybe we can snag him for the V.A. when he finishes his special studies."

"Who knows?" A little smile crept around Alice's lips. "Right now, though, I'd better help Camilla with that turkey, or we'll be eating dinner over in the hospital dining room." She paused. "Not that it would be so bad — Camilla told me they're really knocking themselves out on today's dinner."

Jim watched her go to the kitchen, a strange feeling inside. Then gently but firmly he relocked the door to the past, the door that had threatened to burst when he had turned to the Christmas tree. The past was over. Only the present mattered. Who knew what the future would bring?

It was an odd day. There was brilliant

conversation interspersed with silence. Christmas carols on the stereo. Dinner cooked to a turn. If Camilla was alternately hilarious and sad, no one seemed to notice.

At last Alice Shannon waved good-bye. "I'll be back after the first of the year," she said.

Jim Montgomery went to his room. Marc Butler, his eyes cool, decided to walk over to the hospital again. Camilla was left alone.

There was no need for pretense now. They were all gone. The kitchen was clean, the tree lights low. She was free to go to her own room, the charming bedroom with fluffy white curtains framing the windows and soft yellow walls accenting her own dark beauty.

It had started to snow again, softly, obliterating some of the plowed-up dirty snow on the roads. Camilla didn't notice.

Moving away from the window, where her slender figure had been briefly visible, she turned off her light, threw herself on the bed, fully dressed, and cried herself to sleep. The peace on earth, good will to men hadn't been able to help her. Her first Christmas in Jim's new home should have been so happy! Instead, the only nice thing about it was the fact it was over. Tomorrow she could go back to work. There was no time for aching hearts on a busy hospital ward.

Just before she closed her eyes, she thought of a remark of Jim's from his own fight so long ago. "Thank God for work." Her own lips echoed it now, then stilled. Tomorrow would come all too soon.

Camilla hadn't seen or wouldn't have cared if she'd known Marc Butler had observed her standing by her window briefly. He hadn't stayed at the hospital long. Everyone was tired, anxious to wind down the holiday. On his way back, he noticed light streaming from the window he knew was Camilla's.

On impulse he stepped behind a tree in the yard. He didn't want to be seen. Partially screened, he could see her clearly, shoulders drooping. He could see the weary way she lifted one hand to push back her heavy hair. His professional eye noticed the tiredness, the strain, even as it had during that interminable Christmas Day.

Evidently she wasn't leading an easy life. Gone was the sparkle, the on-top-of-the-world feeling he'd noticed when she first crossed the airport to meet him a few weeks earlier.

His throat constricted. He had seen others showing the same symptoms as Camilla had evidenced since the night he arrived. If they weren't taken care of, they could develop into something serious. He'd have to keep an eye on her. He smiled to himself as her light went out. Sure, all he had to do was keep an eye on her, not to speak of the ward of psychiatric patients. Besides, he wasn't so hot at curing himself of the ridiculous way his heart jumped, even after everything that had happened. What made him think he could help anyone else, especially Miss Camilla Clark?

"Miss Clark." The ward nurse came to her quickly, not running, but getting there fast. "The patient who came in just now — he's dropping blood pressure, fast!"

Instantly Camilla was beside her, heading for the room where the new patient had been put.

"Oh, oh!" Camilla said. "Get Dr. Smith. He's at the end of the ward. Stat!"

In moments the doctor was there, his competent hands probing the patient. Camilla had been unable to see anything wrong with outward signs. Yet it was true. The young man's blood pressure was dropping.

"Here it is." The doctor pressed the patient's side. He was rewarded with a moan. "Nurse, when he came in, what did he say?"

"Just that he felt ill," Camilla said. "Mrs. Kendall was taking the preliminaries when she noticed his blood pressure dropping."

"Call surgery. I think we've got a hot appendix."

Camilla was never so glad to obey as at that moment. She knew if the appendix burst, it would send a flood of poison into the patient's system. Far better to get it out than try to clean up after it burst. Even all the antibiotics there were didn't do the job without a lot of pain and suffering. An infection like that could be stubborn.

"How'd he get past admitting like that?"

"He didn't." Mrs. Kendall's face was grim as she spoke. By now the patient had been sent on to surgery, and the temporary emergency was over, at least for her.

Mrs. Kendall went on. "When he came in, he told that new ward clerk this was his ward. I guess she took one look at him and was so rattled she didn't even think to ask about whether he'd come from admitting. She just sent him in the room. He got undressed on his own, so by the time I got there, he was all ready for attention. The minute I got in the door, he started moaning."

Dr. Smith said, "That's incredible!"

It was. To get into the hospital without

going through admitting was unheard of.

"All I can figure is he must have been on a ward 8 in some other hospital. What with all the pain and fever he managed to find us!"

"Sounds as if we may need to refer him to Dr. Butler after surgery," Dr. Smith said. "Anyone that confused may need some psychiatric help."

Camilla bit her lip but didn't say anything. In spite of her own personal feelings about Marc Butler, she had to admit he was already making a real contribution to the hospital. He was practically indestructible. Reports filtered to the other wards of the hours he spent with his work. Ten, twelve hours a day, followed by staying on call for night emergencies seemed to be his usual pattern.

"You know, I'd think he was doing penance if I didn't know him better," Jim had recently remarked to Camilla.

Her answer had been cool. "Oh? He'd better see he doesn't burn out."

Jim had eyed her but said nothing. He didn't know what had happened over the holidays. He did know all was not well with Camilla and Dr. Butler. It wasn't for him to pry. He couldn't resist adding, "We haven't seen much of him lately."

"No."

They had left it at that.

Later that night, the appendectomy patient was returned to ward 8.

"He's lucky," Mrs. Kendall told Camilla. She had elected to stay on the ward, past her shift, until he arrived. "The appendix burst in the pan."

"Better there than inside him."

"You bet. Good night."

Camilla didn't know exactly why, but instead of sending the regular nurse on duty now to care for the patient, she went herself. He seemed young but couldn't be less than thirty. He also seemed irrational. That was not surprising. There were probably still traces of strong medication in his system. Yet it appeared to be a little more than that.

She stepped back into the hall, undecided, then did what had to be done. Her fingers were a little unsteady as she dialed.

"This is Nurse Clark. Is Dr. Butler on duty?"

A pause followed.

"Dr. Butler, Nurse Clark of ward 8 speaking. I don't like the looks of a patient here. He's recovering from an emergency appendectomy."

"What seems to be the trouble?" Marc asked.

"Nothing definite. Just a feeling I have."

She hung up. He'd be right there. Would he think her foolish? Well, her nurse's intuition told her this patient had other problems besides his appendix. What was his name? Earl Brown. There was certainly more wrong with him than appeared on the surface.

A crash interrupted her thoughts. She stepped back inside Brown's room. He was trying to sit up in bed, wild-eyed. His flailing arms had knocked the water pitcher off the bedside stand.

"Get me out of here," he said. "Where am I?" There was no recognition of anything in his eyes.

Camilla approached the bed, being careful to stay out of his reach. You couldn't always tell how a disturbed patient would react.

"You're in the Auburn Veterans' Hospital. You've had an emergency appendectomy. You're going to be all right." Her controlled voice had the effect of quieting the patient for a minute, and before he could reply, Dr. Butler entered the room.

"Hello, Mr. Brown," Marc said. "What seems to be the trouble?"

Camilla stepped back as he stepped up to the bed. His firm hand was on the patient's wrist with its racing pulse. His air of quiet authority seemed to be helping.

He went on talking. "You're going to be fine. We're here to help you." He motioned to Camilla, then whispered an order for a sedative.

In record time she had the hypodermic ready. At Marc's nod she injected the patient. Marc continued to talk in the same almost monotone voice, and in a few minutes Earl Brown fell asleep.

"That will keep him for a while. I want him transferred to my ward right away." Marc looked keenly at Camilla. "How did you happen to realize he has some emotional problems?"

"Just a gut-level feeling."

"Thank God you listen to those feelings! Too many people push them aside when they shouldn't." He motioned her out of the room and to his office, after the patient was moved. "I have a hunch." He picked up the phone. "Get me the Seattle V.A. Hospital." His fingers drummed impatiently as he was waiting for his call to be put through.

"Auburn Veterans' Hospital here. We have a mentally disturbed patient, an Earl Brown. You have any knowledge of him?" A long pause followed. "I see. Thanks."

He turned toward Camilla, his face curiously set. "Earl Brown was a ward 8 patient in Seattle until this morning. In for observation, complaining of stomach cramps. Something was said. They don't know what. All of a sudden, he knocked down the nurse interviewing him and ran out of the hospital."

Camilla sat down in a hurry. Although she had worked with mentally disturbed patients before, to have one turn up so unexpectedly left her a little limp. "So we got him."

"He must have taken a bus here, been alert enough to know he was getting sicker and needed help. That's why he came on ward 8 instead of going through admitting. I suppose in his confused mind he knew he'd already been through an admittance process."

Marc stood and stretched, then scowled. "How come you're working night shift, anyway? Weren't you on today?"

The concern in his voice got through to Camilla.

"I just felt I should stay."

An unexpected smile broke through the stern doctor's countenance. "Good thing you did. Another nurse might not have been so observant." He scowled again. "Now get home and to bed. You can't work all day and all night, too!"

Resentment filled her. How dare he dictate to her! The feeling was replaced by common sense. He was right. She did manage to say, "Sounds like the pot calling the kettle black. You've been chalking up some record hours since you came here."

"Sure, sure." A gleam of pure mischief came to his face, the first she'd seen since that terrible Christmas fiasco. "Don't tell the timekeeper — she'd have kittens!"

Before she could respond, he was out the door, but his head poked back in. "Remember, go home and get some sleep. And I'll let you know tomorrow how Earl Brown is getting along."

Chapter 8

"Sometimes I feel as if spring will never come!" Camilla said.

Alice Shannon looked up at her sympathetically. The late afternoon sun feebly trying to shine through the window of Alice's office showed the dark circles under the girl's eyes, the droop of the lips usually smiling. "What's wrong, Camilla? Cabin fever?"

"I don't know." She dropped disconsolately into a chair. "It just seems this winter is a hundred years long. I'll be glad when spring comes and we can get outside."

The older nurse studied the pen in her fingers, carefully avoiding looking at Camilla. "How long has it been since you had a vacation?"

Camilla stared at her. "A vacation? What's that?" A reluctant grin crossed her face. "Well, the year before I started nurse's training Jim insisted on shipping me off to the coast for a week."

"I thought so." The quiet brown eyes noted the nervousness in Camilla's fingers, picking at fuzz on her cardigan. "I don't need to tell you the human body can't go on year after year with only work." She raised her hand to still Camilla's involuntary protest. "No matter how much you like that work." She leaned forward. "I'm recommending a week off for you, Camilla, beginning tomorrow."

"A week off? I can't take a week off. There's too much to do. Our ward clerk still needs a firm hand to see she keeps in line. I'd recommend dismissal, but I know she helps support her family. Then Mrs. Kendall just got back from having the flu, and —"

"And ward 8 won't last for one week without you. Camilla, Camilla, what if you were killed? Ward 8 would have to go on." She ignored the stormy protest in the girl's eyes. "Orders. You're to be on leave starting tomorrow." Alice's eyes narrowed suspiciously. "You're also to plan to get out of Auburn."

"You know I can't. Who'd look after Jim?"

For a long moment Alice considered what she would say. When she spoke, her words shocked Camilla. "Jim will live without you. In fact, it might be best if he had to do just that for a few days."

"Alice!"

"Don't 'Alice' me. You can't spend your

entire life taking care of him. You're making him so dependent on you that when you go —"

"Go! I'm not planning to go anywhere."

Again Alice ignored Camilla's outburst. "Of course, you are. You may think now you'll never marry, that you'll spend the rest of your life taking care of Jim. You can't do it, Camilla. You'll both become old and disillusioned. Someday you'll marry, when the right man appears."

"Some chance."

Alice pretended not to hear the bitterness in her voice. She wasn't so blind as it seemed. In the weeks she'd been at the hospital she had kept her mouth shut and observed a lot — such as how Nurse Clark never raved over the fine work of a certain Dr. Butler as the other nurses did. Alice was wise enough to keep her own counsel.

In her earnestness, her eyes became direct, piercing. "I'll ask you again, Camilla. Suppose you were killed? What about Jim then?"

"I suppose he'd have to manage without me." She was on her feet, eyes blazing. "But why should he have to manage without me now? Just so I can get off somewhere for a vacation? Or is it a rest cure?"

"Perhaps it is. I don't like the way you're

on edge, Camilla. It's only a matter of time until it affects your work."

"I'll never let personal problems affect my work." She regretted her statement immediately. "That is, if I ever have personal problems."

"Good. I'll speak to Dr. Montgomery about your leave right away."

"I suppose you've even planned what I'm supposed to do."

"As a matter of fact, I have." Alice laughed at the blank look on Camilla's face. "I still have my Seattle apartment. I'd like you to go there. It has a fireplace, a well-stocked refrigerator, a shelf full of good books, a television, a stereo. It's close enough to theaters and shops for you to get out; far enough away to be fairly quiet for a big city. I want you to rest. There's a park across the street. I want you to walk, every day."

"Yes, Mother."

Alice laughed. "Enough of that."

She stood, but not before Camilla asked suspiciously, "Did you say well-stocked refrigerator? How come?"

"Oh, I've been thinking of sending someone there for R & R."

"Rest and recuperation." Camilla sighed. "Okay. But what about Jim?"

"You don't dress and bathe and feed him, do you? He's really quite capable of managing on his own. He eats here, not that it would harm him to learn some cooking. All you really do is be there when he wants you." Alice's eyes softened at the misery in the girl's face. "I'm sorry, Camilla, but you have to get away. And it's not going to hurt Jim, not for a week. You can call him nights."

She wasn't prepared for Camilla's question.

"Why don't you ever talk about Dr. Jones?"

For a moment Alice refused to meet the other nurse's steady gaze, then she smiled. "Oh, Dr. Jones."

"Yes. Dr. Jones. Your fiance. Don't you miss him? You seem to be completely happy in your work here. What are you going to do when he comes back and wants to get married? Isn't it going to be hard on you? You don't really think your Dr. Jones will want to join our staff, do you?"

Alice sat back down. Suddenly she looked old, tired, drained. "There is no Dr. Jones."

It was Camilla's turn to drop back in her chair. "What?"

"There never has been a Dr. Jones. There never will be." Lines of pain filled Alice Shannon's face.

"But why, Alice?"

"More than anything in the world I wanted to help Jim, in whatever way I could. It was the only way he'd allow me back in his life."

Her frank admission left Camilla speechless.

"You realize this must not go out of this office," Alice said.

Camilla nodded. She was still too stunned to speak. When she finally did get her voice back, it was to demand, "Then all this time, you've just been waiting for a chance to get back to Jim?"

For a moment pride warred with honesty in Alice. Honesty won. She said, "Yes."

Seeing that Camilla couldn't grasp it, she explained. "It didn't matter to me that we had never actually taken our wedding vows. From the time I met and fell in love with Jim, I was his as completely as if we were married. For better or worse." Her calmness threatened to crack, but she swallowed hard. "That's how it is, Camilla. How it's always been. How it will always be."

Camilla's mind was whirling. To love like that. It was almost beyond comprehension. "But you — you could have a normal married life. Have children. Don't you want that for yourself? You're still young."

For a moment Alice drew aside a veil,

giving Camilla a glimpse of her innermost heart. "There are millions of men and children. There's only one Jim. I would rather be married to Jim Montgomery, share as much of his life as I could, than anyone else in the world!"

The dam broke, letting out the flood of feeling that had been locked behind it for years. "Camilla, I only wish we had been married before the accident. Then nothing on earth could have kept me out of Jim's life! We weren't. There's nothing I can do. If he even suspected the real reason I took this job, he'd dismiss me immediately. He must not know."

"Never?"

Alice's lips trembled, then settled into their own firm line. "Never." This time there was decision in her face. She walked to the door and opened it. "I'll expect to see a more rested nurse on ward 8 a week from now. In fact, I think I'll go speak to Dr. Montgomery about it right now." Her tone was brisk. The veil was back in place.

But as Camilla stumbled down the hall, fighting the tears behind her eyelids, she knew she had met a person beyond belief. She thought, *If ever I'm tempted to give up on life, I'll remember this moment. I think I've experienced hard things. Compared to Alice, my life has been easy.*

Her thoughts were still jumbled over dinner that night. It was another of those rare times when she and Jim could be home together.

Jim brought up the subject. "Alice Shannon tells me she's giving you a week off."

"Ordered is the word."

Jim put down his coffee cup and grinned. "So maybe she's right. I've noticed how pale you've been lately. I think she has a good idea."

"What about you?"

He looked surprised. "I'll be fine." He grinned again. "Of course, I'll be glad to eat your cooking after a week of hospital food, good as it is. Perhaps it's the atmosphere."

Camilla deliberately set a light tone. Alice had been right. Jim didn't really need her. It had showed in the way he answered. "You can think of me all tucked up cozily reading and listening to the stereo while you slave!"

"Maybe Prince Charming will come around and take you out."

"What's that supposed to mean?"

"Don't act coy. You know half the doctors in the hospital, to say nothing of the other hospital employees, would be camping on our doorstep if you gave them an ounce of encouragement. What happened to Dr. Butler?"

"The psychiatric wonder boy?" Instantly Camilla knew she'd gone too far.

Jim highly resented criticism of any of his hand-picked staff.

"I was referring to Dr. Butler."

"Sorry, Jim. I guess I just don't care for his type." Before he could answer she had slipped out of the room, leaving him staring after her.

What had Marc Butler done to incur her wrath? Whatever it was probably wasn't any of his business. On the other hand, anything affecting Camilla affected him. He wheeled his chair down the hall. She was standing staring out the window of her room.

"Want to talk about it?" he asked.

At first she shook her head. Then a longing to throw off her burden welled up inside. She tried to keep her voice light. "He doesn't approve of my living here."

"He *what?*" Jim's brows pulled together until a sudden thought hit him. "He knows you're my sister, doesn't he? Everyone else in the hospital does, although it's never really discussed."

"Not to my knowledge."

"Well! I'll certainly set him straight first thing tomorrow."

"Don't you dare!" She whirled from the window. "If that's what he chooses to believe, don't you dare tell him any different! We shared some time together, even discussed ideas and ideals. If he hasn't any more faith in me than to believe . . ." Her voice broke.

Jim involuntarily made a sound of sympathy. So this was the result of his bringing Marc Butler to Auburn. Camilla was in love with him. "I won't say anything. But I think you should. When he first came, I believe he cared a lot for you, Camilla."

Her heart leaped. Jim was too obtuse about love matters to notice until hit in the head with a board. Marc Butler must have shown some very evident symptoms for him to be aware of anything. She stubbornly shook her head. "What good is it for someone to care if they don't have any trust? I've seen too much of so-called love. If there's no mutual trust, and respect, and honor, then it isn't worth anything."

"I don't want you to become bitter about love, Camilla."

"Why not? The divorce rate is so high a person only has about a fifty-fifty chance of even keeping a marriage together. And how many of them who stay together are really happy? Better to stay single and out of trouble."

Jim turned from her to look outside. Darkness fell early. All he could see was waving branches outside the window. "Yet for those who are willing to work, willing to give, marriage can be heaven." A tinge of color crept over his face. "I want you to marry, Camilla. I want you to have children, learn to laugh with them."

"And you?"

"I have my work — and my memories." Sadness replaced the color in his face.

Instantly Camilla was contrite. "I'm sorry." She buried her face in his lap as she had done when she was a child.

His hard hand stroked the dark hair. "Don't be. All of us face many things. I've always felt it isn't so important what we face, as how." He lifted her chin, looking into the tear-stained face. "Things have a way of working out. Not always the way we want them. But still they work out." He saw the cloud, the doubt in her face.

"I've never really spoken of how it felt to know Alice wouldn't be part of my life the way we'd planned. I think it was almost harder to overcome than my actually becoming a wheelchair patient."

"But it was your choice!"

Pain crossed his face, the same pain Camilla had seen in Alice Shannon's face earlier that day. "There was no other choice."

"Wasn't there?"

"Of course not." He stirred restlessly, impatiently, in control of himself again. The moment for sharing was nearly over.

Cam seized it before it slipped away. "What about Alice?"

"She has found someone who'll make her happy, give her everything I couldn't. Children, everything she'll want."

"I wonder."

For a moment doubt filled Jim Montgomery's eyes. He brushed it aside. "The past is over, Cam."

"I know. And the future may never come. What counts is now. If you've ever drilled anything into me, it's that."

His eyes filled with relief. Camilla was on her way back to her normal state of happiness. He hadn't seen how she'd lost her sparkle until Alice mentioned it today. He'd been too busy.

"Well, I'll get out of here and let you pack," he said. "Don't forget to throw in something pretty. Prince Charming may still appear."

"If he does, I'll tell him only a coach and four will be good enough for me." She was determined to meet his lighter mood. There had been enough seriousness that night.

Long after Camilla slept, Jim lay with his hands behind his head, thinking. Camilla had been hurt about what Marc believed. Or did he really believe anything at all? No, Camilla was too sharp to overlook even hidden feelings. Yet she hadn't been sharp enough to see how Marc Butler had fallen for her almost immediately.

Was it his own fault for keeping her so close to him? He thought of the scrawny kid she'd been, the protective feeling he'd always had for her. He'd tried to replace the stepdad who'd loved her as his own daughter. Maybe he'd kept her tied too close to him. Alice had hinted at it that afternoon, telling him Camilla needed a life of her own.

Alice. For a few moments Jim allowed his past feelings to override the planned course he'd chosen. If things had only been different. They weren't, never could be. With the forced ability of the trained doctor who knows he must rest, Jim shut off his mental thought processes and slept. There was always tomorrow to consider Camilla and Dr. Butler.

Besides, he had more or less agreed to keep out of it. He was too busy to play Cupid, even if he wanted to, and he wasn't sure he did. Jim had overcome nearly all of his earlier negative feelings toward Marc. And Marc Butler was an outstanding doctor and psychiatrist — but a husband for Camilla? That would take a lot more thought.

The hospital grapevine was busy the next morning. During the night, one of the psychiatric patients had escaped. No one seemed to know how. Dr. Butler hadn't been on duty. The other doctor and nurses hadn't seen him leave. But the fact remained that Earl Brown had somehow managed to get away.

Dr. Butler was furious as he demanded, "How did this happen?"

There were no apparent answers. More important, where had the man gone? In working with him, Marc had recognized some pretty deep symptoms. He could, on provocation, become dangerous. Where was he?

A search of the hospital was made. There was no trace of him. The hospital guards hadn't seen anything out of the ordinary. The bus driver who regularly stopped in front of the hospital had picked up no passenger fitting Brown's description.

"He has to still be on the grounds," Marc said, worried.

"Not necessarily," Jim said. "He could

have simply slipped away in the dark." He noticed the drawn look on Dr. Butler's face. Marc was having a rough time of it. "Can he be dangerous?" Jim asked.

"Under aggravated conditions, I feel he has the potential to be dangerous. Let's hope he doesn't get aggravated."

"I've called the police. The Auburn City Police cooperate with us beautifully. Once he's gone from the hospital compound, he's their problem, too."

"Good." Marc thought for a moment. "You know, I want the ward 8 personnel to be alerted. He might try to go back there. In his confused state, it's hard to tell exactly what's in his mind." He hesitated. "Miss Clark will recognize him."

"She isn't there. She's taking a week off, going to stay in Seattle, do a little shopping and a lot of resting."

"When was she leaving?" Marc asked.

"She's probably gone now. She'd called an old friend and was going to meet her for lunch." Dr. Montgomery checked his watch. "Eleven o'clock. Yes, Camilla's gone."

A premonition of something not quite right fluttered in Marc. He started to brush it aside, then remembered telling Camilla, "If more people would listen to their gut-level feelings, they'd be better off." He walked to the window. "That's strange. Her car is still in the driveway."

Jim followed him to the window. "It sure is. I wonder why?" The two men's eyes met.

Marc was the first to speak. "I'll go see if she's in the house."

"Take the keys." Jim tossed his house keys to Marc, then stood at the window watching the tall doctor sprint across the street.

Marc knocked, waited, rang the bell, called, "Camilla. Miss Clark, are you here?"

No answer. He tried the door. Locked. He opened it and stepped inside, disappearing from view.

When he came back out, he relocked the door and walked around the house. No Camilla. When he came back to the parked car, he tried its doors. All locked. He could see clothing inside, neatly hung on the rack. Evidently she was all ready to go.

But why had she locked everything up, then disappeared? Had she gone across to ward 8 to check on some last-minute detail?

"No sign of her," Marc said. "She's all packed." He was breathing hard as he came back to the hospital director's office.

"I don't like this. I don't like it at all." Jim reached for his intercom. "Get me ward 8. . . . Mrs. Kendall, has Miss Clark been in this morning? . . . Yes, I know she's on leave.

Just thought she might stop in first. . . . What? A call for her, earlier? I see. Thanks."

He turned back to Marc. "She hasn't been there, but a call came in for her earlier. From the domiciliary ward. Mrs. Kendall told them she wasn't on duty today. The nurse said she'd call her at home."

Jim already had the domiciliary ward on the line. "I understand there was a call for Miss Clark from your ward? . . . Yes, thank you."

He put down the phone. "Elizabeth Wakefield, a friend of Cam's, seems to have disappeared. Engineering called and said she didn't come in for her work. And she wasn't in her room. No sign of anything strange. The nurse knows Camilla has taken a special interest in Elizabeth. She thought maybe they were together."

Marc stared at him. "We're getting quite a few missing people, aren't we? A psychiatric patient. A domiciliary patient. The head nurse on ward 8. Something's going on."

Jim gripped the arms of his wheelchair. "We've got to get to the bottom of this — and fast!"

Even in his own concern, Marc noticed the deep lines beginning to etch themselves in Dr. Montgomery's face. How much he cared for Camilla Clark. The pain and fear on his face were reflected in Marc's own.

Now was no time to stand there medi-
tating about anyone's feelings. The important question was: Where was Earl Brown?
And Elizabeth Wakefield? And, especially,
Camilla Clark?

Chapter 9

Once Jim had left for work, it didn't take Camilla long to straighten up and get ready to leave. She backed the car out of the garage and packed it. She was in her coat ready to go out the door when the phone rang.

"Hello? . . . Oh, Elizabeth. . . . No, I can't get together this afternoon. I'm going to be away for a week. . . . Seattle. . . . Sure, I'll be happy to do an errand for you."

Camilla glanced at her watch. It was still early. "Why don't you run over before going on duty? On second thought, I'm all packed. I'll meet you halfway. It's so nice outside, I'll run down the walk back of engineering and meet you by the warehouse. You can tell me just what you want. . . . Oh, sure. You can give me the money, too."

She hung up, locked the door, and slipped down the sidewalk behind the buildings. As if to make up for its former sullen appearance, the day had become bright, almost springlike. Camilla straightened her shoulders. It would be good to get away. She smiled at the thought.

Once she had been convinced she was really to go, anticipation had done the rest. She was looking forward to her holiday. She'd just loaf, not do anything she didn't want to. When she got back to the hospital, it would be with a brand new perspective.

"Hello, Elizabeth!" A warm feeling went through her. She had learned to love Elizabeth Wakefield. Her earlier compassion had grown to appreciation. Despite her heart condition, Elizabeth was doing well, working when she could. The woman was happy, needed. That was the clue, Camilla thought. Everyone needs to be needed.

"Maybe we'd better step inside," Elizabeth said, trying to hold her hair against a little breeze and reach in her purse at the same time.

They moved through the great doors of the warehouse. Camilla shivered a bit. It was so big, shadowy in the far corners. It always gave her a funny little feeling. Where were all the warehousemen? Must be on early coffee break.

"Now what I'd like you to do is match a scarf to this piece of material —" Elizabeth broke off, realizing Camilla wasn't listening to her.

Camilla was staring at a man who had stepped from the shadows. He was not a warehouseman. He was a patient. His clothing showed that. A little chill ran up Camilla's back. Where had she seen this man, this trembling person with the wild eyes?

Then she said, "Hello, Earl Brown. What are you doing here?"

The challenge in her voice brought hatred to the man's face. He lurched closer, his big hands working convulsively. "I'm getting out of here." His smile was nothing short of a leer.

"Where are you going?"

"Who cares? Away. Going to get away from here." He had gone over the brink from sanity to madness.

It took every ounce of courage Camilla possessed to answer him calmly. "Oh, I wouldn't do that. You can be helped here. Isn't Dr. Butler helping you?"

A cunning look chased away the hatred. "Yeah. Sure. Doc Butler." He looked both ways and whispered, "He's going to put me away. Put me in the loony bin." He cackled. "Not old Earl. Too smart for him. Too smart for all of them."

If only she could keep him talking. Camilla smiled and leaned forward, hating the smell of his breath, the glazed look in his eyes. He was dangerous, or could be. Behind her back she motioned for Elizabeth to back away. If only she could get help! The warehousemen would be back in a few minutes.

"Of course, you're smart," Camilla said. "So smart you got out of the ward." She forced a laugh. "How did you do that, Earl?"

He laughed foolishly, not seeming to notice Elizabeth inching her way backward. "Smart. Earl's smart. Waited until night. I stole the doctor's coat. Got out when some other poor guy was brought in. No one saw me."

Crash! Elizabeth had backed into a small hand truck. Even her instinctive grab hadn't prevented it from falling.

Instantly the man whirled toward her. "Where you going?" He grabbed Elizabeth's arm. "Trying to get away from old Earl, huh?" He shoved her back to Camilla.

Head up, he listened. In the distance there were voices. "Get in there!" Earl snapped, jerking them into a small closetlike enclosure stacked to the ceiling with boxes. There was barely enough room for the three of them.

"If you make one sound, you're dead," he hissed in their faces.

For a moment Elizabeth hesitated.

Camilla squeezed her hand hard, whispering, "Do as he says."

A grin crept across Brown's face. "Thatsa girl. Nobody gets hurt. Just do as old Earl says."

The voices came closer, then receded. Evidently the warehousemen were working at the far end of the building.

Brown froze in place as one of them called, "Hey, Pete, how come this hand truck's turned over?"

"Don't know. Someone must have knocked it over."

Then there was silence punctuated only by a faraway laugh now and then.

"What are your plans?" Camilla asked. If she could just keep him talking, he might relax a little. She watched in horror as he pulled a shining, razor-sharp scalpel from his pocket. How on earth had he managed to get that?

As he talked, he ran the edge along his thumbnail, grating against the nail, filling the temporary prison with fear.

"Plans. She wants to know my plans." He spoke to the scalpel as if it were alive. "Going to get out of here."

"But what about us?" Elizabeth couldn't help asking.

"Hostages." He grinned at their surprise. "Been watching TV. Ever'body gets hostages. Me, too." He leered at them again. "Might even take you with me."

Elizabeth's fingers bit into Camilla's arm, but she said no more.

"Why not just me? You don't want two of us," Camilla said.

"Shut up. No more talking." He waved the scalpel. Huddling into a ball, he stared at them, his eyes unwavering.

Camilla and Elizabeth moved closer together, sitting on a box. Was it minutes or hours the silence went on?

Once Elizabeth ventured to whisper, her lips barely moving, "We'll be missed."

Her words produced another gleam of hatred in their captor's eyes and a menacing wave of that scalpel.

I would take a chance if it weren't for Elizabeth, Camilla thought. She called on every bit of knowledge she had of mental disturbances. She had been taught in nurse's training to keep her voice low, to at least pretend to go along with those who were insane. It did no good to argue. Sometimes a quiet, seemingly calm acceptance of the situation could settle down a disturbed patient.

But Elizabeth is a patient, too. I owe her protection, Camilla thought. Yet she knew that at least for the moment there was nothing she could do. Not while he had that scalpel. He could hurt them both terribly or even kill them.

For a space of time Camilla debated calling out, alerting the men at the other end of the warehouse. She couldn't do it. While Elizabeth might get away, she couldn't take the chance.

Now and then Camilla sneaked a glance at her watch. The hands seemed frozen. How soon would they be missed? When Elizabeth didn't report in at engineering, they would probably call the domiciliary ward. When Jim noticed her car was still in the drive, she would be missed.

Earl Brown was sure to have been missed early this morning. How had he hidden? Surely the entire grounds must have been searched. Somehow he must have evaded the searchers. He was clever. Too bad he wasn't just crazy. His flashes of rationality provided him with the ability to reason just what to do next.

Hostages. TV. The senseless seizing of innocent victims in order to protect criminals, or those wanting something. She had never thought she would be a hostage. She had agonized over the plight of those taken, never knowing what it was really like. Now she felt cold fear, sitting a few feet from a man who was playing with a lethal instrument.

She shifted about, cramped from sitting in one position. "May I stand and stretch?" she asked.

He nodded grudgingly, curling himself more into a ball. If only he would drop that scalpel.

"That's enough!" he snapped.

She dropped back to her place by Elizabeth. Thank God for Elizabeth's calmness. After the older woman's one outburst, she had been still. She was frightened. It shone in her eyes. But she didn't by word or deed cross the man. Was she thinking much the same thoughts as Camilla? Probably.

Were the minutes creeping by while Elizabeth retraced the events of her morning? Of course. Camilla caught Elizabeth's eye. She didn't dare smile. It might anger Brown. She did manage to look at Elizabeth steadily. Something passed between them and both were strengthened.

The hands on Camilla's watch stood at five minutes before twelve when voices outside their cubicle pierced their consciousness.

"Hey, Pete! Ward 8 needs a case of tissues. I'll get it out and we'll deliver it after lunch."

Heavy steps came close. Camilla felt as if her heart would stop. *What would happen*

143

when the warehouseman opened that door? Would Brown attack him? The man wouldn't have a chance. Unprepared, he'd fall before Brown's fury. The door started to open. Slowly, slowly . . .

"Door seems stuck." The man couldn't know Brown was shoved against it.

"Aw, let it go until after lunch. I'll help you then," his friend said.

"Okay by me. Let's go eat." The steps faded, disappeared.

Camilla, Elizabeth, and Earl Brown were alone.

Camilla's hands were wet with perspiration. She hadn't realized she'd been holding her breath, ready to scream before she'd let the warehouseman be attacked. Maybe this would be their chance. When they came back, there would be two men. She thought rapidly. If only they could divert Brown when the lunch break was over!

She hadn't counted on the return of a completely lucid moment for the man with the scalpel.

"Come on," he said. "We're getting out of here!" He jerked the door open, stood staring into the warehouse, then slammed the door shut — but not before one of the men outside had seen him, the scalpel, and the two women huddled together behind him.

Earl Brown made no effort to control his curses. They were horrible.

"Pete!" the first warehouseman called.

There were heavy footsteps, silence, and then the sound of many feet.

"Camilla!" a familiar voice shouted.

"Marc!" Nothing on earth could have kept the cry back.

Even Brown's heavy hand over her mouth, his ordered, "Shut up!" didn't still her.

"He has a scalpel!" she shouted. Marc mustn't break in here, he mustn't! Brown would hurt him. Better for her to die than the man she loved. Loved!

"You witch!" Brown growled, holding the scalpel over her.

Camilla could see Elizabeth moving toward them from her corner. But before she could reach them, Brown swung his arm, strengthened by fury and fear, knocking her down. She fell hard, her head hitting a packing box.

Camilla could see the trickle of blood start and shouted, "You've killed her!" Maybe it would shock him to his senses. It didn't.

"You're next!" he said. "But not yet."

They could hear the door creaking on its hinges. In another moment it would give way. When it did, Marc Butler stood in the doorway, appalled at the sight before him. Elizabeth Wakefield lay on the ground. He could see even from his position she wasn't badly hurt. Head wounds always bled a lot. She needed attention but would most probably be all right.

But what transfixed him was the scene against the back wall of the little storage area. Brown had one arm around Camilla, pinning her to him. The other arm was held higher, clutching the scalpel near her throat. "One move, Doc, one move and I carve her!"

Marc froze in place. He couldn't chance Brown's hurting Camilla. The silence lengthened. He had to do something, say something. His voice was hoarse. He couldn't get a word out. When he did, it amazed him.

"You're the boss, Brown. Okay if I help her?" Marc motioned to the prostrate Elizabeth, his eyes never leaving Brown's.

For a long moment they just stood there. Then the sheer command of Marc Butler overrode something in the weaker personality.

"Go ahead," Brown said. "But one move —" The scalpel finished the sentence.

"She'll be all right." Marc stanched Elizabeth's blood flow. Already the old woman showed signs of regaining consciousness. That must not happen. She might scream, might trigger off Brown into another rash act. "Okay if we get her out of here, Brown?"

Again there was an exchange of glances. Then Brown said, "Yeah. Hate the sight of blood."

Marc Butler had to bite his tongue to keep back the wild wave of hysterical laughter that threatened to choke him. A moment later he thought of the significance of Brown's words. If he hated the sight of blood he would probably only use the scalpel on Camilla if he was deliberately provoked.

"Get her out," Marc said, indicating Elizabeth.

The warehousemen had a stretcher. By the time she was carried out, her head had stopped bleeding. She would have a king-sized headache, but probably no other ill effects. Luckily, her heart condition did not appear to be affected by what had happened. But what now?

There was an interruption at the warehouse door. "You can't go in there!" a guard said, barring someone's way.

"Who says I can't?" The demanding voice

almost broke Camilla's control.

It was Jim at the door, Jim demanding entrance. Jim, who was fair game if the warped mind of Earl Brown ever saw the opportunity afforded by a man in a wheelchair.

"Keep back!" Marc Butler's warning voice broke through her rising panic.

Dr. Montgomery had managed to get past the guards but was in the back, out of sight of Brown. Something in Marc's authoritative voice stopped him. "Is Camilla all right?" Jim asked.

"Yes." The single word conveyed a world of meaning to Jim. He remained motionless. Something in the stance of Dr. Butler reassured him more than anything else could have done. Strange, if he had had to choose a man to help him right now, Dr. Butler would be that man.

"All right, Brown. Let her go." Marc's words chilled Jim Montgomery to the core.

Was Marc crazy? Had his faith in Dr. Butler been misplaced? Impulsively, Jim started forward. The motion of Dr. Butler's hand stopped him. Marc had felt rather than seen Jim's movement. Nothing must interfere, nothing.

"You crazy?" Brown said. "She goes with me."

Marc Butler didn't budge an inch. "What do you want with her? Women get in the way. Remember? You told me that. Always a woman, getting in the way."

Brown didn't answer, but Marc never took his eyes off the man. Inside, he was praying for help, praying to know what to say to get this troubled man to release Camilla. Nothing mattered now except her safety.

"Remember how it was, Brown?" Marc went on. "You could have made it big. They kept you back. Your mother. Your wife."

Camilla gasped. How did he know all that? Oh, of course. Through his working with the man now holding her, the man who might kill her or maim her for life.

The doctor's quiet voice continued. "Always in the way. Slowing a man down. Even in the service. Remember the girl at the base? Always wanting, asking, grasping. You don't want this one, Brown. She'll slow you down. Keep you from the big time."

His voice was almost hypnotic. Brown's face began to work. He was remembering. Remembering how it had been. The doc was right. Always a woman. Always in the way. In quick revulsion, he threw Camilla from him, across the little enclosure, against the wall of packing boxes.

Marc Butler's eyes never left him. "Good, Brown. Good. Get the women away from you. It'll give you a chance to be somebody." He paused, letting his words sink in.

Camilla thought her heart would stop beating. What would Marc do now? She was free, at least temporarily. Intuition told her not to move, not to call attention to herself in any way. The battle was not over. The next moments could be the most dangerous of all.

"Now the scalpel, Brown."

Camilla pressed both hands to her mouth to keep back the cry of horror.

Marc Butler was advancing. Step by cautious step. Fearless, curiously white, he approached Brown, his hand out. "Give me the scalpel, Brown." Another step.

Camilla closed her eyes. She couldn't bear the suspense.

A small stick on the floor snapped from Marc's weight. Camilla's eyes opened. He was still there, coming toward Brown.

"No!" Brown jerked away, cowering against the wall. "No!"

"Give me the scalpel, Brown," Marc persisted. "It's time for lunch. You'd like that, wouldn't you, Brown? You didn't have much dinner last night. Too busy stealing a coat. Making plans. You're pretty smart,

Brown. Even got the scalpel. But you're hungry. You had no breakfast. It's been a long time since you had food."

Marc could see Brown's mouth work. "It's fried chicken today, Brown. Fried chicken and whipped potatoes. Green salad. Apple pie. You like fried chicken, don't you, Brown?" He took another cautious step forward. "Remember? Remember how you told me your aunt used to fry chicken and make apple pie?"

Brown automatically licked his lips. He seemed to have forgotten the scalpel. Marc deliberately took another step, smiling now. "You can't eat holding that thing, Brown. You have to have a fork. A big plate of chicken and a fork. Can't eat holding a stupid scalpel."

Brown looked down at the instrument in his hand. A puzzled frown crossed his face. Why was he holding the scalpel? "Fork," he said, holding out the scalpel to Marc.

From her position by the packing boxes, Camilla prayed. This was the important moment. It could go either way. As Marc Butler accepted the scalpel, Brown's fingers tightened, then released the instrument.

"Come on, Brown, let's go eat." Marc handed the scalpel to an openmouthed warehouseman, motioning back the guards who had stepped forward with handcuffs. With his arm about the slighter man's shoulders, he continued to talk. "We have to go back to the ward, Brown. They won't know where to find us out here."

And, docilely, the would-be murderer let himself be led away.

"Follow them closely, just in case!" Jim Montgomery's snapped order to the guards released Camilla from her shell of ice.

Awkwardly she got to her feet and stumbled over to Jim. The impact of recent events had taken its toll. She reached Jim just as a wave of sick, hysterical laughter overcame her.

"Camilla!" Jim was shaking her.

It didn't help. She only laughed harder. "It's so funny, Jim. Dr. Butler took the big, bad man's toy away. It's so funny."

There was pain in Jim's voice as he said, "It's shock. She's been through too much. Get her to bed."

Camilla was only vaguely aware of white-uniformed nurses, a sterile-smelling lotion, something rubbed on her arm, then a pin-prick. She didn't feel like laughing anymore. It wasn't funny. *Elizabeth?* she wondered. *Where was Elizabeth?* Camilla must have cried out her question.

"She's fine, Miss Clark. She's just fine," a nurse said.

Someone had called her Miss Clark before. Funny, she couldn't remember. Was it Dr. Butler? Hadn't he done something for her? She felt fuzzy. Her tongue was thick. She was in a strange room now. She couldn't talk. She had to help him. She couldn't let go. But who did she have to help? Jim? Was Jim in the hospital?

"She's wandering. It's the effect of the drug," the nurse said. There were people in her hospital room. Jim. Why was he in a wheelchair? He had come home from Vietnam safely. They'd been so glad! There was Alice. Camilla tried to call out, ask Alice to stay. No one could hear her.

It was night now, just a little light. There were people in her room again. Who was in bed? Was that Jim? Oh, yes, there had been a terrible accident.

What are you doing in here? The words ran through her head.

Was she supposed to answer? Jim had asked the question. Had they caught her hiding in the bathroom? What had happened to the young soldier with the bandaged head?

Someone was speaking.

"You've done it, Marc. You said once

you'd give your life for me. You could have today. I couldn't have done what you did."

What was the other man saying? Why did he look so familiar? His back was to her. His words were muffled. "I had no choice."

"My world could have ended today in that warehouse," the first voice said.

"You care that much." It was a statement, not a question.

"I always have. From the day her mother married my father. Cam was just a little kid. I'd never had a sister. Now she was mine, all mine!"

"Your sister!"

"Yes, my stepsister. But I love her like a sister."

"And that's why she lives with you?"

"That's why she lives with me. When the folks died, all Cam and I had left was each other. And since Alice had gone away . . ."

But Alice hasn't gone away, Camilla wanted to cry. Alice is here. She's always been here. Why couldn't she move, speak, make them listen to her? What was wrong with her, anyway?

No, she mustn't speak. They mustn't know she was hiding in the bathroom, near Jim's hospital bed. They must never know. Jim would be angry. They would all be angry that she had sneaked into the hospital

154

where she didn't belong. She mustn't ever tell anyone, not even Jim.

But why did they go on and on like this? Her head hurt. If only she could sleep. Maybe it was all a bad dream. It probably was. She'd just sleep and when she woke up, Jim would be home and they'd do all the things they'd planned.

It was almost time for Jim's wedding. She was going to be a bridesmaid, Alice had promised. They would shop for a dress soon. Mom and Dad would be so proud — Mom and Dad? Where were they? Oh, yes, they were home. They didn't know she was hiding in Jim's room. She mustn't tell.

"She said not to tell." Was that Jim speaking again? If only they'd all go away, even Jim! She needed rest.

"I've done a terrible thing. Can you ever forgive me?"

Those words sounded almost familiar. Why did they bring back memories, half complete, frightening? What terrible thing had this person in her room done, this man whose back was to her?

Was this the man with the bandaged head? Had he done something to Jim? Something to put Jim in a wheelchair for the rest of his life?

With a mighty effort, Camilla fought to

throw off the smothering blanket holding her from them. She understood now. Marc was the man who had caused the accident that had crippled Jim.

"You! It was you all the time!" she gasped. But the long strain had been too much. She could not get through.

A lone tear escaped from her eye. She had tried so hard. Now there was nothing left to do but sink into oblivion and darkness.

Chapter 10

Spring had finally come. It had not brought the happiness Camilla Clark had hoped for. She had been up and around in a few days, outwardly showing no particular signs of trauma. Inwardly she was torn. She sat on the porch of the hospital director's quarters watching Alice Shannon weeding daffodils.

"Pretty, aren't they?" Alice asked, sitting back on her heels. "I always look forward to the daffodils."

"Alice." Something in Camilla's voice caught at the older woman's heart. "Am I having a nervous breakdown?"

Alice considered for a moment, then shook her head. "No, Camilla. Not exactly."

"Then why can't I remember everything that's happened?" There was a tormented look on her face. "I try so hard and —"

"That's part of the problem." Alice abandoned her work and dropped to a chair near Camilla. "For a long time you've carried a heavy load, Camilla. Too heavy. Starting with the worry over Jim when you were a teenager and he was in Vietnam, there hasn't been a time you have been able to let your mind rest. He came home, the accident occurred. You hadn't fully adjusted to that when your folks died. You kept on bravely, but the mind can only stand so much."

"I remember all that. It's just more recently that I can't remember. I was supposed to take a vacation, wasn't I? Didn't you tell me to take a vacation? I don't think I went wherever I was going. Where was it, Alice? Why didn't I go?" Her hands were locked in her lap. "Why can't I remember? Did something terrible happen to me?"

"Not exactly." Alice remembered Dr. Butler's orders: *Don't force her. Let her remember naturally.* "Don't worry about it, Camilla. When your body and mind are ready for it, you'll remember."

Camilla rubbed her head. "I know. Patience. But you don't know how hard it is not to remember." She changed the subject. "When can I go back to work?"

"Not for a while. Camilla, you're what is called a fatigue victim."

"You mean like battle fatigue?"

"Similar. Human beings can only stand so much. Then they have to break. If you had taken your vacation, this might have been averted. On the other hand, it might merely have been postponed. No work for you until you're thoroughly rested, young lady!"

"Alice, when are you going to tell Jim there really isn't a Dr. Jones?"

The words floated clearly through the spring air, through the open window, to the ears of a man who had been studying at a desk inside. Jim's head snapped up, the color draining from his face. He strained to hear Alice's quiet answer.

"I don't know. I had hoped never to tell him. He might send me away. Lately I've wondered if he suspected." Her eyes gazed absently across the flowerbeds. "Oh, Camilla, if he could only see how much I need him!"

The poignancy of her cry was not lost on the suffering eavesdropper. Neither was his sister's answer.

"I think in a way Jim's being selfish, Alice. He's so afraid you'd come to despise him for not being the man who first asked you to marry him, he isn't thinking of what he's doing to you. I know. He probably thinks he's being noble, saving you from being tied to a man in a wheelchair. He really thought you'd find someone else. But you haven't."

"No. And I never will."

Despite the years of self-imposed control, Dr. Jim Montgomery's truant heart missed a beat. Alice loved him! She had always loved him! He missed a little of the conversation.

Then he heard Alice say, "Camilla, do you know Dr. Butler has a friend who is working with a new technique to restore mobility to spinal cases such as Jim's?"

"No. How do you know?"

Alice took a deep breath. "I overheard Marc talking to Jim. He asked Jim how long it had been since he'd had a thorough examination or X rays of his spine. Jim told him a long time, too long to get his hopes up on some new technique."

Camilla was intent on Alice's words. Neither of them saw the curtain flutter as a tortured man in a wheelchair moved closer to the window. "What did Dr. Butler say?" the girl asked.

"He said it was still an experimental process. It might not work or come to anything. But if Jim would consent, he would ask that doctor to fly here and look him over. Jim said no."

"No! Why?"

"He said he was resigned to being where he was. It would only be worse to get everyone's hopes up, *especially yours, Camilla,* then have them shattered on merely a promise."

Camilla's cry would have reached the

dead. "No! He mustn't feel that way. If there's even a chance, he has to take it. Not for my sake, but for his own — and yours."

Jim couldn't stand it anymore. He rolled his chair to the front door and through it. The two porch occupants gasped. Neither had ever seen him like this.

"I'll thank you to keep your hands off my life," he snapped. "It's my life, isn't it? I have the right to do what I choose."

For one awful moment Alice Shannon felt like sinking through the ground. He had obviously overheard the entire conversation. Then with a spurt of courage she didn't know she had, she stood and walked to his wheelchair. "James Montgomery, I have known you a long time. But I never knew you were a rank coward!"

"Coward! Now wait a minute!"

"You wait a minute." Alice's gentle brown eyes blazed with fire. "I've waited for years. I let you shove me out of your life because you thought it was for my own good. I stood back and watched you make a fight a lesser man would have abandoned before it started. I kept hands off, because it was *your life!*

"Well, let me tell you something, Dr. Montgomery, no more. It's not just your life. It's Camilla's and mine. I'm not standing back while you convince yourself it's all foolishness. You'll either take that chance Dr. Butler told you about or you're the worst kind of coward in the world!"

Her voice broke. Alice turned and ran across the street to the hospital, leaving absolute silence behind her.

"Bravo!" Dr. Marc Butler caught her as she ran blindly. He hadn't heard all the words but the clear air had carried enough of them to him for him to grasp the subject of her outburst.

"Oh, Marc!" Alice clung to him, sobbing. "What have I done? He'll hate me for this."

"Would you take it back?"

His question brought the fire back to her eyes.

"Never! I meant every word!"

"Then it isn't the end of the world." From his pocket he produced a spotless handkerchief. "Come on. Smile for the guy."

Alice's smile was a little wobbly, but she did feel better. "I guess from your standpoint, this has been building up for quite some time."

"For many years, Alice. I think you know that."

Her eyes filled again. "I've hardly cried since the day he told me he didn't want me in his life. But now that there's a chance, no matter how slim, for him to get out of that wheelchair —"

"I know." Marc looked above her head, across the street.

Dr. Montgomery was beckoning.

"Alice, I think we're being summoned," Marc said.

"I can't go back, not now."

"If you don't go now, you never will."

Silently Alice followed Marc across the street, back to the porch. She refused to look at Jim or Camilla. Yet what she had told Marc Butler was true. She wouldn't recall her words if she could.

There had been too many years of heartache, followed by the deception about Dr. Jones. Now it was over. No more leaving unsaid those things that should have been out in the open years ago.

"Dr. Butler, I want you to tell me again about your friend," Jim said, his face grave.

"I can't promise a thing. He will have to come, examine you, and then make a qualified guess as to whether this new technique could be successful. I do know it has worked with others."

Marc wasn't prepared for Camilla's icy accusation.

"Don't listen to him, Jim. He's just trying

to hurt you again, like he did all those years ago!"

Too late Camilla remembered she wasn't supposed to know anything about that time or Marc's late-night visit to Jim's hospital room. It didn't even slow her down. In her state of mind she could only remember this was the man she'd longed to meet for years, to tell him what he had done to her life as well as Jim's. "Oh, yes, I know all about it."

She ignored Jim's stern, "That's enough, Camilla."

And she directed all the hurt of the years toward the white-faced young doctor. She didn't even see Alice shrinking back, her hand to her mouth. All Camilla saw was Marc Butler, the man who had left Jim a cripple.

"I was there," she said. "In Jim's room. No one knew I had gone there, but it was my brother in that bed. I saw you come in, Marc. I saw you look at Jim with your bandaged head and see what you'd done. I heard everything you said."

"Then you must have heard me forgive him." Jim's voice was harsh. "You also must have heard him promise to take up my dream and make it come true. He's done that, Camilla. He's also done much more than that. If it wasn't for Dr. Butler, you would have —"

"No, Jim," Marc said. "Not now. She has to confront the past first." He faced Camilla squarely. "It's true, it's all true. But you don't know me as well as you think, Camilla Clark. Do you know of the years of regret I've had? Do you think it's been easy knowing that because of a drunken act, the finest man I've ever known was consigned to a wheelchair? Do you know of the black nights when I was tempted to turn back to the same alcohol that created my problem, then shuddered and fought memories on my own?

"No. You wouldn't know about those things. Maybe you wouldn't even know how I came here when a part of me probably didn't want to. Seeing your brother in a wheelchair every day was like rubbing sea water in an open sore. But I was needed. I could never make up for what I did. At least I could come when Jim asked me."

Marc drew a ragged breath. "I meant it when I told him I would give my life. Now there's a possibility he can walk. Just a possibility. But I'd give everything I own for that one chance. I intend to see he gets it, despite what you think. I've already called Dr. Seagrave to come."

Marc met Jim's indignant eyes. "Sorry, I

165

had to do it. I thought if he were here, you might relent."

Camilla felt as if her heart had been pulled up by the roots. Jim was shocked, pale. Marc Butler was totally colorless. What had she done? She had opened a Pandora's box and the porch was filled with ugliness.

"Do you think I'm a coward?" Jim's question brought Camilla back to reality.

She closed her eyes and swallowed hard. She had to think what to say. It could make a difference forever.

Slowly Camilla opened her eyes. "No, Jim, you aren't a coward. But I think you're going to have to face things — the same way I am." Her voice was gentle, almost a whisper.

Would no one ever speak again? Camilla looked around the little circle. Alice, white and still. Marc Butler. He had said what he had to. Now he waited. Jim . . .

As if he read her mind, Jim turned to Marc. "All right. I will submit to the examination." He didn't seem to hear Camilla's little cry of relief. "On one condition." His eyes sought Alice's. "If the examination proves favorable, and if the new technique works, will you marry me?"

There was a moment of stunned silence.

Then Marc held out his hand to Camilla. There was no place for them in this discussion. Quietly they slipped through the door. But the window was still open, the porch conversation clearly audible in the still air.

Alice looked at Jim, the man she'd loved for so many years. For one moment her lips trembled. Then she spoke. "No, Jim. I won't marry you if the new technique works."

Inside the living room, Marc put a hand across Camilla's lips to stifle her outcry.

Alice walked across to Jim, still in his wheelchair. "If I'm not good enough to marry you now, for better or worse, then I won't marry you when you can walk again."

Jim's face turned even whiter. "You mean . . ."

"Exactly. I'll marry you now, as soon as we can get our license and put in our waiting period. Otherwise, I'm going to walk out of this place, pack, and go so far away you'll never find me."

"You're being melodramatic, Alice."

"Am I? Then perhaps it's time. Your stubborn pride has kept us apart for a lot of years. Don't you think I have pride, too? That's my ultimatum. Trite as it sounds, it's going to have to be now or never."

Behind the curtain, Marc Butler had removed his hand from Camilla's mouth, but the arm across her shoulder was like a vise. She could hear the clock ticking off the seconds. No matter how long she lived, she would remember this moment, standing there waiting for her brother's decision.

It came. "All right, Alice. What kind of wedding do you want?"

There was a rush of feet. A smothered, "Jim!"

This time Marc led Camilla to the kitchen. She stumbled, but the strong arm supported her until she could drop into a kitchen chair. She felt drained.

"Well, that's that." Marc sat down opposite her. "A little belated, but a happy ending nevertheless."

"How can you joke about it?" Camilla stared at him, her dark eyes brimming. "All these years and —" She swallowed a sob of pure nervousness at the look in his eyes. All those years. She remembered what those years had meant to Marc.

"Camilla, what do you really see when you look at me?"

His question caught her off-guard, unprepared. To gain time she pretended to take his measure. "A dark-haired man in a white doctor's coat and three pens in his pocket."

She dropped the pretense as she saw his eyes blaze. He was in no mood for joking. "I see a man who has suffered and been mis-judged." Sudden tears stung her eyes.

It took all Marc's self-control not to clutch her to him. "You missed something."

Her dark eyes met his.

"You should have seen a man who is very much in love with you."

"What!" Color drained from her skin. A little flare went off inside her, but she refused to recognize it. "After everything's that happened?"

"After everything's that happened." Should he remind her of the hostage incident? No. She had to learn to care for him without it being a matter of gratitude.

"But you can't expect that I could ever love you back!"

"I don't expect it. I only can hope." He forestalled all the objections growing in her eyes. "I know. You feel you owe loyalty to Jim. You feel you can never forgive me for what I did, even though I was unconscious at the time of Jim's actual accident. But, Camilla" — he stood and stepped to the kitchen door — "if Jim can forgive me, and he has, maybe in time you can also forgive. All these years you've carried the burden of what you overheard in the hospital room that night. That's one of the reasons you're having some trouble now. A load of hatred or resentment can get pretty heavy after such a long time. Isn't it time to put it down?"

Long after he had gone, Camilla sat at the table. He loved her. She alternated between a warm glow, and remembrance of him as he had been so long ago. Perhaps the Marc Butler who had returned from Vietnam didn't even exist. He certainly bore little resemblance to the Dr. Marc Butler of the hospital staff.

When Jim and Alice finally came inside, the house was still. Alice found Camilla asleep on her bed. The excitement had been too much for her. There was so much to grasp. Alice stood in the doorway looking at the girl who would soon be her sister.

"God grant you the happiness I have found," Alice said, then closed the door and went back to Jim and the beginning of a new life.

It was a solemn yet joyous little group who gathered in the hospital chapel a few days later. Alice and Jim had decided to be married by the chaplain.

"The newspapers would have a field day with this if we had a big wedding," Alice had said. "Why not just have a few of the hospital personnel?"

She looked beautiful in the off-white

dress she had chosen. Never had Dr. Jim Montgomery looked so handsome and proud. They would spend a few days in Alice's Seattle apartment, then be back at the hospital in time for Dr. Seagrave's visit.

Only snatches of the wedding ceremony penetrated Camilla's ears. In pale yellow she stood with Alice, welcoming her as a new sister. Once her eyes met Marc Butler's and an errant thought crossed her mind. He would be gentle, tender, a good husband.

Camilla dropped her lashes to hide the thought. Since he had told her he loved her, she had thought of little else. Sometimes she was still torn by loyalty to Jim. Other times she knew Marc Butler was more like the Mr. Right she had waited for than any man she had ever known.

Hot tears stung Camilla's eyes as Alice stooped to kiss Jim at the end of the ceremony.

Maybe in a short time she wouldn't have to stoop. Yet the radiant woman who lifted her head was not to be pitied. Alice's serenity would hold, no matter what the future might offer.

"Do you want me to move somewhere else?" Camilla put the question point-blank to Alice, who had been back from her honeymoon only a few hours and was arranging dishes from the dishwasher in the cupboard.

"Sure, when you get married." Alice's impish grin reassured Camilla more than anything else could have done.

"I just thought since it's your honeymoon still, at least sort of . . ." Camilla stammered, feeling herself turning red.

Alice stopped what she was doing. "It's not a typical honeymoon, Camilla. We aren't a typical family. After all we've been through, we may never be considered typical. But as long as you want to live here in your own home, I'll be proud to have you."

"I'm sure glad you finally beat some sense into Jim!"

This time they both grinned.

"Just like the Royal Mounties, they always get their man!" Alice's smile died as she saw the effect of her words on Camilla. "What's wrong?"

"It's just that Dr. Butler told me he's in love with me."

"I know. He has been from the time he first met you. He told me when he looked up and saw you crossing the airport terminal he knew you were special." A look of pity filled Alice's face. "Don't you remember any of it, honey?"

"No. Not about him coming or about what

happened when I was supposed to be on vacation. Why, Alice, why can't I remember?"

"Marc says it's because you'd had so much unhappiness, your mind refused to recognize any more. After all, he's the doctor." She turned back to the dishes. "He says it will come back, will be triggered off by some little incident."

"I wish it would happen soon," Camilla said.

"When we get through with Jim's tests and all that, we'll work on it."

Alice's promise seemed vague. Camilla could sense she was concerned about Jim's future. Even then he was undergoing the preliminary tests.

When he came home that evening, his eyes held a mixture of emotions. "Well, it's worth Dr. Seagrave's time trying."

"You mean he wants to go through with it?" his wife asked.

"Yes." Jim looked first at Alice, then at Camilla. "He wants me to clearly understand that even if the technique is successful, it doesn't mean I'll be one hundred percent okay. There was too much permanent damage. What it does mean is that my spine might still be stiff, but I would be able to walk, slowly. I would have to use a cane, especially at first. I'd never be able to play tennis or that kind of thing. But there are many things I could do."

He grinned. "In other words, the miracle would be a little miracle. But I'd get out of this." He touched the wheelchair.

"I think that's a pretty big miracle all in itself." Camilla said.

"Me, too." Alice grinned. "Of course, the first miracle was getting this big oaf to marry me." Her twinkling eyes took the sting out of her words.

"Yeah." Jim had had enough of the glooms. "Anyway, I'm scheduled for tomorrow." He wheeled his chair toward the bedroom. "He doesn't believe in waiting, that's for sure."

Waiting. It seemed like hours that Dr. Butler, Camilla, and Alice waited while the surgery was performed.

Alice had insisted on being on duty in the recovery room. When she came out to Camilla and Marc, her face glowed. "He's coming out of it. Dr. Seagrave says there's every reason to believe he's going to be all right. It's like we were told. He won't be as good as new, but he will be free of his wheelchair. Thank God!"

Something stirred in Camilla as she looked at Marc. She had never seen such a

174

look of joy on a man's face. What it must mean to him, she hadn't considered until this moment.

She turned away. It was too much like looking into a naked heart, and she knew that, at least at this point, she wasn't prepared for what she would find hidden in Marc's.

Chapter 11

"Camilla, how much are you willing to go through in order to remember?" Jim asked.

His question stopped Camilla's breath, but only for an instant. "I would give anything I own." She watched him for a moment.

He no longer sat in a wheelchair. He was stiff and it wasn't always easy to get up and down, but at least he could walk. It was so much more than they could have hoped for.

"It might not be easy," he said.

"Were things so bad, my mind refused to accept them, as Dr. Butler says?"

"They were frightening. Coming on top of everything else, they proved to be too much. But now that I'm back on top of things, that should be a help. All of the past except the last few weeks has taken care of itself, Camilla. Now I think you're ready to face everything."

"How?"

It was characteristic of her brother not to mince words. "Dr. Butler wants you to relive the day you were going on vacation." He saw a shadow drop over her face. "He's convinced it's the best way for you to remember."

Camilla laughed, but it was only a shaky effort. "Funny, I feel scared already, and I don't even know what to expect. I'm not going to be hurt, am I?"

"No!" Jim's answer was explosive. "Nothing will hurt you, Camilla. Nothing!"

"I believe you. When do I start?"

"Tomorrow morning if that's all right with you."

She took a deep breath. "Fine. The sooner, the better." But part of her was crying out, *No! I don't want to have to remember something hurtful.* The more sensible side of her nature realized her memory loss had gone on long enough. It was time to face everything.

"Is Dr. Butler part of it?" she asked.

"Very much so." Jim's voice was grave. "He will be here to tell you what to do. Don't be afraid to trust him, Camilla. He wants what's best for you. He loves you a great deal, you know." It was the first time Jim had discussed it.

"Don't you mind?"

Jim looked surprised at her question.

But she went on. "I mean, if someday — maybe — I cared for him. Would it bother you, after all that's happened?"

Jim stepped over to where she sat and looked down at her. "I would be more than proud to call Dr. Marc Butler my brother-in-law, if it ever comes to that. Yes, he made a terrible mistake when he was younger. He's paid for it ever since. That's over, Camilla. The future is what counts. I can think of no man I would rather see you marry."

Something inside Camilla relaxed. She had felt torn since the day Marc had told her he cared. She had fought her own growing feelings, telling herself that because of Jim she must never let herself care. Now that obstacle was gone, wiped away by the sincerity in her brother's voice.

From a corner of her mind came Marc's words: *A load of hatred or resentment can get pretty heavy after such a long time. Isn't it time to put it down?*

He had been right. She felt free, light. From deep inside bubbled a happy laugh, the first Jim had heard from her in a long time.

"All right, Doctor. We'll bury the past, grab the present, and let the future take care of itself!"

"Not quite. You have tomorrow to live first."

"Don't be so grim, Jim. It can't be that bad!"

★ ★ ★

But it was. By the time Marc Butler came for Camilla the next day, her hands were wet with perspiration. It did no good to scold herself, ordering herself to calm down. After all, she was a nurse. She shouldn't be frightened by merely reliving a specific time period in her life. Dr. Butler was an expert in such things, and he would be with her the entire time.

"Ready, Camilla?" There was compassion in Marc's dark eyes.

"As ready as I'll ever be." She locked the car door after putting her things in it as she had that day. She locked the house door and followed Marc down the walk. "I still don't remember anything, you know."

"You will." His face was set. This was a calculated risk. When Camilla remembered what had happened that fateful day with Earl Brown, she would also remember the misunderstanding between him and her, how he had doubted her.

Yet it was a chance he had to take. Before it could develop, Camilla had to face the past, all of it. Marc prayed she would be able to stand it and forgive him.

Just before they reached the warehouse area, Marc stopped her. He laced his fingers through her own, holding her in a firm grip.

179

"Camilla, remember. Whatever happens, I'm right here with you." A pulse beat in his throat. "I won't leave you alone."

"Camilla, over here!" A woman was standing near the warehouse door.

Camilla stared, at first not recognizing her. Then she said, "Why, Elizabeth! Elizabeth Wakefield!"

Marc held her hand as she hurried toward Elizabeth. It was working, at least the first part of it. If only Elizabeth could carry out her part of the program.

Elizabeth's face was white. She knew a great deal depended on her. "Here's the money, Camilla, and the fabric. Be sure to get a scarf that will match." The old woman smoothed her hair. "It's windy out here. Let's step into the warehouse."

Every trace of color drained from Camilla's face. "No!" Her voice was shrill. "We can't go in there!" Remembrance of another day was glazing her eyes. "He's there!"

"Who is there, Camilla?" Elizabeth forced herself to move closer to the door. She mustn't let them down now. Dr. Butler had told her how important it was for Camilla to enter the warehouse and actually see where they had been imprisoned.

"Elizabeth! Come back!" Camilla wrenched free from Marc and raced after her friend, her own fear forgotten in the fear for Elizabeth Wakefield. Her mind clicked. She had done this before. Her heart threatened to choke her as she stepped into the warehouse. Off to one side was an open door. A man in hospital clothing was forcing Elizabeth into the little storage room.

"No!" Camilla flung herself against him, pounding him.

"It's all right, Camilla." Marc Butler held her.

"He has a scalpel." Fear for Marc forced the words from Camilla's tight throat. "Don't let Marc come in! He'll die, and I love him."

Strong arms gathered her close, let her sob against a strong chest. Somewhere she could hear a drum beating, or was it a man's heart? "Marc, thank God you're safe!" She shivered in his arms. "I thought . . ."

"It's all over. See?" He turned her toward Elizabeth, who was smiling, crossing to her, tears running down her face.

"But Earl Brown —"

"Has been safely put away where he can be helped and where he won't be bothering anyone else." Marc noticed Camilla's eyes riveted on the man in hospital clothes. "Pete, come here."

Camilla's eyes opened wide. "Why, you're

one of the ones who helped us!"

The man looked sheepish. He had hated the part he'd just played. If it hadn't been for Dr. Butler insisting, he couldn't have done it. Yet seeing Camilla standing there now was worth it. "Pretty good actor, huh?"

"Almost too good." She shuddered. "Marc, I want to see in that little room."

He hesitated.

"I insist. If I don't, I'll never pass this warehouse without being frightened."

Silently Pete slid the door open. Camilla stepped inside. Everything was the same. She and Elizabeth were inside. Marc and Pete were in the doorway. No, it was not the same. There was no wild-eyed man with a scalpel. Elizabeth was standing near, perfectly whole, not lying on the floor with a head wound. There were neatly stacked boxes, a well-swept floor. Just a storage room, nothing more. There was nothing here to dread.

"Oh, Elizabeth!" Camilla turned to her friend, her tears mingling with Elizabeth's. "How terrible it must have been for you!"

"For me?" Elizabeth was stunned. "What about you?"

Camilla's eyes were clear, unshadowed by the past. "But all this time you must have lived it over and over. I haven't been able to remember until today."

She looked toward Marc. "Thank you." Her simple words caused even Pete to rub his eyes. She was so lovely as she stood there, the last horror of memory fading from her eyes. She was gallant, courageous. If Marc had loved her before, now he felt as if his feelings had intensified by a hundred percent. She was everything he had always wanted — and someday she would be his. He would do everything in his power to see to that.

"Well, our little drama is over." Marc nodded to Elizabeth and Pete. "It couldn't have been acted out without you. I'll have to sign you up as assistants."

"Not me. I'm a warehouseman," Pete grunted and grinned.

"Me, neither. I'd better get to my clerical work or they'll be calling the domiciliary." Elizabeth smiled, patted Camilla's hand, and walked off.

"She's a far different lady from the discouraged one who came to us last fall." Camilla watched her go. "I guess that's what being needed does for a person."

The little room was empty. Marc pulled the door closed and turned to Camilla. "Maybe this isn't the time to ask you, but, Camilla, I've loved you since you met me in the airline terminal the night I came. Will you marry me? I'll make a real home for you."

Camilla felt flooded with joy. Marc loved her, really loved her! Jim approved. There was no reason she shouldn't say yes.

"Camilla, you're such a beautiful person. Not just outside, but inside. Like the song says, 'I can't promise you a rose garden,' but I can promise to love and cherish you all my life." He sensed the stiffening in her. What had he said wrong? He couldn't know that, with his comment, something else had come to her mind.

A snowy night, a walk around the hospital, and then his words: *Thank you for wearing my roses, Miss Clark.*

Camilla's face turned white. She backed away from him. "No, no, I can't marry you." She looked miserable. What had frightened her? He'd been so sure she'd respond, after her desperate cry during the little stage play.

"It's Jim." Marc's tone was flat. She couldn't forgive him for what had happened many years ago. There was no other explanation.

"Not really. It's you. You didn't trust me. I remember now. 'Thank you for wearing my roses, Miss Clark.'" Her voice was a perfect mimicry of his on that wintry night. "Do you think I could ever marry you after that? I remember now. I even tried to tell you on Christmas morning — no, the day before. Or sometime around then. But you wouldn't listen."

"Do you think I haven't regretted it every waking moment since?" His fingers bit into her arms, just as they had done that morning by the Christmas tree. He was colorless, intent. His eyes blazed.

"I have never learned to control my temper. I should have known by the kind of person you are that, no matter what the situation looked like, you would be true. Camilla, my only excuse is that I was already in love with you, and insanely jealous of a man I'd ruined. When I found you lived in his house, I felt as if the world had ended. In the dark hours I figured it out. You must be his wife. Yet if so, why . . ."

He couldn't go on, couldn't explain he had wondered why she had returned his farewell kiss. In her mood, it would be disastrous.

Camilla denied the hot blood racing through her veins. He loved her that much! But he hadn't trusted her. It hurt, more now than it had even then. Suddenly she wanted to hurt him more than anything in the world, to hit out at him.

Her eyes were cool, her smile mocking, as she said, "Please, Dr. Butler." She raised her hand. "If you don't mind, I really find this whole conversation rather boring. Now if you'll excuse me, I think I'll walk back home."

The look on his face frightened her. Had she gone too far?

She wasn't prepared for the way he caught her close, pressing his lips against her own. She was too surprised to struggle at first. Then she pulled back. It was to no avail. His arms were stronger than steel, pinning her to him.

When he finally released her, her lips burned. She cried, "How dare you? I hate you for this, you know!" Tears of weakness from what she had gone through were followed by sheer fury.

It didn't even touch him. He leaned back against the packing boxes. "You'll have to admit, it was fun while it lasted." Ignoring her sputtered protest, he surveyed her, almost coldly. "You might keep in mind just one thing. In some countries there is a tradition that when someone saves your life, you belong to that person."

He turned toward the door, then back. "Just remember, I've always been a firm believer in tradition. Watch your step, Camilla

Clark, or I may turn caveman and carry you off one of these days."

The door slammed behind him. Camilla was alone.

"I hate him! I'll always hate him!" Memory of his kiss sent fire through her veins. How could he treat her like that?

Be fair, Camilla, part of her urged. *He has told you he loves you. He knows you clung to him when you thought of that day with Earl Brown, and that you realized you loved him. He even proposed to you. Why shouldn't he kiss you?*

"I did love him," she told the packing boxes defiantly. "But now he's ruined everything."

The result of Camilla's journey to the past, as Jim called it, was that she went back to her ward the next day.

"I'm perfectly all right," she told the nurses. "Once I realized it was all over, I was fine."

She had given them an account of the incident, carefully leaving out anything to do with the emotional impact or quarrel with Marc Butler. He was such a precious human being in their sight they would probably stick up for him.

"Dr. Butler does wonders in his field, doesn't he?" Alice was all smiles, thrilled that Camilla was back to normal. She wasn't above doing a little matchmaking, either. "He's quite a guy."

"I suppose so. He's qualified for his work. But then, anyone who specializes in a field has the advantage over a general practitioner."

Alice looked at her, surprised, but said nothing. If Camilla still held some coolness toward the doctor, Marc Butler himself would have to change that.

Camilla was glad to get back to her work. She had missed seeing her patients, hearing the friendly and sometimes not so friendly hospital gossip.

It was on her third day back she got a real piece of news.

"Hey, heard about Dr. Butler?" Mrs. Kendall was speaking to Dr. Smith. They were just outside Camilla's office.

"Sure have. He's getting all fixed up in his quarters. One of the other doctors asked him what was going on and he told them he thought he'd be getting married pretty soon."

"You could sure have knocked me over with a feather when I heard it. I'd thought he and Camilla . . ."

There was sudden silence outside her door, as if the speakers had just become aware it was partially open.

"Well, back to work," the nurse said.

Footsteps sounded in two directions, but Camilla hardly heard them. Marc Butler fixing up his quarters? So he thought he'd be getting married pretty soon. What could it mean? Surely he didn't think it would be to her! But who else?

A terrible thought crept into Camilla's mind. What if he had some old girlfriend from somewhere? Maybe when she had turned him down so hard, Marc had contacted another woman. So who cared?

I do. Camilla ached all over. If Marc married someone else, her life would be meaningless. She thought of his tall darkness, his strength to lean on when she had faced that second time in the warehouse. She remembered his kiss, his telling her practically point-blank that she belonged to him. Could he have forgotten in just a few days? She had heard about the fickleness of men, but she hadn't thought Marc would be like that.

Why not? She had turned him down and hard. No man would ever forgive the way she had talked to him, especially after having thrown herself in his arms and declaring her love. Her face burned even remembering it. The fact she was having a hard time was no excuse. She should have been able to handle it without coming unglued all over him.

If he marries someone else, I'll go away, she decided. But it was a long time after the overheard conversation before Nurse Camilla Clark could pick up her pen and finish the stack of reports on her desk.

Chapter 12

"Miss Clark, I don't like the way the patient in bed five looks." Mrs. Kendall's usually calm face was worried. "I wish you'd have a look at him."

Camilla looked up from her reports with surprise. It was unusual for Mrs. Kendall to seek out help. She was a top nurse, extremely competent. If she was concerned, there must be reason for it.

"I don't know why I have this feeling about that particular patient, but something seems to be wrong."

"Has Dr. Smith seen him?" Camilla asked.

"Only briefly. He read the chart and was just beginning to talk with the patient when he was called to the phone."

Camilla had seen a lot of patients in every condition, but nothing like the one in bed five. He was conscious but evidently unable to speak. He pointed to his throat. His face was beginning to darken.

"Get Dr. Smith immediately and bring a tracheotomy tray!"

Dr. Smith was there almost instantly,

along with Mrs. Kendall and the instruments. There was no time to waste, no time to get this man to surgery. He was choking badly.

Dr. Smith took the shining scalpel, opening the trachea. A great rush of air went into the man. Immediately his color lightened, but the nurses were too busy with sponges to notice.

"Here it is!" Dr. Smith held up the culprit, a small fishbone. He was soon busy closing the wound. His heavy eyebrows bristled. "Good thing you noticed right away."

"But how could he have a fishbone?" Camilla asked. "It's been an hour since lunch!"

"Don't know. It must have been in his throat and worked itself down." Dr. Smith looked down at the patient. "He'll be fine now, but I'm curious as to just how he could have that bone in his throat and not know it!"

The mystery wasn't solved until later. When the patient recovered and could talk, he looked shame-faced. "It's my own fault. I love fish. I couldn't eat everything that was served at lunch, so I kept back one of the fish." He looked at them apologetically. "I didn't know if the nurses would like it, so I decided I'd better go ahead and eat it. I stuffed it in my mouth when I heard her coming." He nodded to Mrs. Kendall. "She must have seen something was wrong."

"She sure did, and it's a good thing for you!" Dr. Smith was stern. "In the first place, our food service is careful about bones, but once in a while even the frozen ones will turn up with a bone. I hope this is a lesson to you."

"It is. I don't like fish anymore."

It was all Camilla could do to keep from roaring with laughter. She managed to get out the door and back to her office along with Dr. Smith and Mrs. Kendall.

"He learned a lesson, all right," Camilla said. "He doesn't like fish anymore!"

They rocked back and forth, letting out emotion. It wasn't often they had the chance. A hospital was no place for hysterics. Yet something this funny was just too good to forget, especially without first getting a normal human enjoyment from the situation.

Dr. Smith wiped his eyes. "You know, if medical personnel couldn't laugh once in a while, they'd probably explode!"

"I agree." Mrs. Kendall was blowing her nose, still chuckling. "Well, we'll have to see that patient isn't served fish anymore!"

A new world started for Camilla the next

day. She had decided to take night shift for a while. As ward supervisor head nurse, she had the responsibility for ward 8. She wanted to see how the night shift personnel were doing, so she had decided to spend a full two weeks with them. There was another reason for the change in shift that only Camilla knew.

There had been too many sleepless hours since she had overheard the scuttlebutt about Dr. Butler's remodeling his quarters. By working nights she would be too exhausted not to sleep the next morning. It would give her time to adjust to knowing Marc Butler would share his life with another woman.

If she felt resentment at the thought, it did not help to justify herself. She had had her chance — and ruined it. Because of her being hurt by his attitude, she had put him off. Now he evidently had found someone else, someone who wouldn't mock him.

It would be better this way. There was little chance she would see him when she was on night duty and he worked days. If he still spent night hours in his psychiatric ward, it didn't matter. It was a long way from ward 8 to Dr. Butler's domain.

The first week slid by. Camilla was pleased with the change. Even as she had predicted, she was so tired by the time her shift was over, she had no time to brood. It was a different world, quite in contrast with the day shift. Camilla found herself on top of her paperwork load for the first time in ages.

She also found she was of assistance, perhaps more so than on day shift. Not in the more pressing needs, but in other more subtle ways. The first opportunity came only a few days after she started her new schedule.

About four in the morning Camilla had sent a night nurse for a break. "I'll watch the ward."

She was unprepared for the way the night nurse's face lit up.

"Gee, that would be great. Usually, I just grab a cup of coffee at the desk. Even though it's a pretty quiet world, a person is still on duty. You never know when a patient will awaken and want something."

The ward was quiet. But before the other nurse returned, Camilla heard a soblike sound. Was there a call light on? No. Yet there was a sound. On rubber-shod, quiet feet she walked the length of the ward, especially checking the doorways of the private and semi-private areas.

At last she found it. The muffled noise

was coming from the curtained-off area of a semi-private room. She stepped inside, being careful not to shine her tiny flashlight beam directly on the patient. "Anything I can do to help?"

She picked up the chart, noting the male patient was listed as forty-four, in for a series of tests. The man was turned away from her, curiously still now that she was in the room.

"Mr. Classon?"

"I'm all right." But the hoarseness in his throat belied his words. A moment later he asked, "What would you do if you were just about at the end of your rope?"

A hundred thoughts crossed her mind. There was nothing on his chart to prepare her for the despair in his voice. Even hospitals couldn't know the entire background of their patients. For only a moment she hesitated, knowing how important her answer would be, how rigid he lay waiting for what she would say.

Automatically her hand pushed the heavy hair back from the feverish brow.

"Why, I think I'd tie a knot and hang on until things got better."

Was it imagination or did he relax a bit? She smoothed his pillow, smiled at him in the dim light. That human touch softened him.

"I suppose you think I'm an awful baby, in here blubbering."

"Not at all. If men would let their feelings out, there would be a whole lot more men alive!" She deliberately kept her voice calm. "Society has done a grave injustice by teaching that little boys don't cry. We get them in here all the time, little boys who didn't cry and have grown into men who don't. Heart attacks, all kinds of pressure. Frankly, I would like to see strong men cry when they need to. There's nothing babyish about it." She could feel him relaxing as she straightened his sheets, tangled into a mess. Finally she asked, "Do you need someone to listen?"

"Someone to listen! When have I had that?" Mr. Classon drew in a deep breath. "You probably don't have time for me."

Camilla thought rapidly. If she left, even to go to the doorway and make sure the night nurse was back on the ward, her opportunity might vanish. He needed her now, not five minutes from now. She was relieved to see the other nurse appear in the doorway. Camilla motioned to her to let her know all was well. Good. The ward was covered.

"I have all the time there is."

He was quiet so long, she wondered if

he'd forgotten she was there. When he did speak, the despair was back in his voice. "I don't even know where to start."

Camilla was too wise to push. She settled down in the chair by his bed, close enough for him to know she was there, far enough away not to be threatening. "Wherever you like."

"My wife wants a divorce." There was such deep pain in his voice, Camilla flinched in spite of herself. "We've been married over twenty years. We've raised two kids. They're in college now. Last week she tells me she's decided she wants a divorce."

"And you don't want one?"

"No! I've loved her since I first saw her in pigtails. We moved next to her family when she was about ten. We went together all through high school. Got married on graduation night. I've worked hard, provided a good home. Now she's leaving me."

"Did she say why?"

His answer was more of a groan than a reply. "She says I can't really love her or I'd trust her." It was a red-hot thrust into Camilla's own heart. Her silence encouraged his confidences. "When the kids were gone she decided she'd like to work, at least part-time. She got a job in an office. One night the boss drove her home. I saw her laughing, getting out of the car. Something inside me snapped. When she came in, I accused her of wanting to work just to get out of the house, away from me."

Another long silence followed. "She laughed at first. Said she couldn't believe her ears. It made me angry. I told her either she quit the job or else.

"She just looked at me. The next day she quit the job. I thought everything was okay. Then last week she says she's thought it all out. A divorce seems to be the only answer."

Oh, ye of little faith! The Biblical quotation ran through Camilla's mind. First Marc, now this unhappy man. For a moment angry words trembled on her lips. In him she could see Marc. Both were unable to trust the woman they loved. She bit them back and substituted, "Mr. Classon, have you said you're sorry?"

"Yeah. She said if I really meant it, she would feel differently. I can't make her believe me. What can I do? How can I make her believe me? Nurse, you're a woman. What would a guy have to do to make you believe him?"

From somewhere in Camilla's training came a remark from one of her instructors: "Remember, when you're dealing with women, you're dealing with little girls who have grown up. It's different with men. You're dealing with human beings who still retain much of the little boy. They need reassurance. Your own maternal instincts will help you handle the little boy in the grown men you serve."

The question had been put straight to her. What would a guy have to do to make you believe him? What would Marc have to do? She closed her eyes against the rush of pain that swept through her. Why hadn't she believed him? Why had she let him find someone else? Most important, what could she say to Mr. Classon?

As she spoke, her voice trembled a bit, then steadied. "I think a guy would have to be patient and give me time. I think he would need to show me he trusted me, and not just tell me."

"Then you think my wife won't divorce me?"

"I don't know, Mr. Classon. I only know she's been hurt, really hurt at your lack of trust, at your unfounded jealousy. It's tarnished something she has held as precious and shining for over twenty years. It will take time."

A big work-worn hand covered her own. "Thanks, Nurse." His voice was husky again.

Instantly the woman in Camilla receded before the nurse. She stood, checking the chart. No medication was called for.

"Mr. Classon, try and get some sleep. Things always look worst in the middle of the night."

"Okay."

She started toward the door but he stopped her with a question.

"Nurse? Would you talk to my wife, if she's willing, that is?"

What had she gotten herself into? Was she some kind of marriage counselor or something? Yet how could she refuse? "I'll talk with her, Mr. Classon."

He dropped back, satisfied. This nurse seemed pretty sharp. Maybe she could help. Funny, all the worries about the tests seemed to have settled down. Maybe there wasn't too much wrong with him. His stomach had been tied up in knots ever since the big argument with Marie.

Now things seemed to have smoothed out. Why had he been such a fool? Marie was the most wonderful person in the world, the most faithful. If only she would listen to this nurse.

"That nurse" slept far less during her rest time than Mr. Classon had. She had promised to meet with Marie Classon the next afternoon. Long before the appointed time, she was back in uniform and on the ward.

She had tried to think what to say. She had been tempted to confess to Jim or Alice what she had let herself in for but knew how they might react.

She could just hear Jim roaring, "You are no trained psychiatrist! Hands off the patients' personal lives!"

Better not to even tell him what she planned to do. What that was, she didn't know — not until she saw Marie Classon.

Mrs. Classon's face was white when she stepped in the office. "Bob said you wanted to see me. He isn't seriously ill, is he?"

"No, he isn't. All the test results aren't back in, but it appears most of his trouble is being aggravated by nervous tension."

"Thank God." The pleasant-faced woman sank back in her chair. "I thought —"

"It's all right, Mrs. Classon. Things are going to be fine." She wondered how to approach the subject of their family problems. There was no way to do it but come right out with it. "Mrs. Classon, your husband mentioned things aren't going too well at home."

Tears welled up in Marie Classon's eyes. "No, they aren't, Miss Clark. Ever since Bob threw that insanely jealous fit, I've felt as if I were walking around in a glass cage.

Numb, and as if at any minute the whole thing might shatter." She looked directly at Camilla. "I love my husband, but if he doesn't trust me, even after all these years, what do we have left?"

"I think he realizes how wrong he was. I don't suppose he will tell you I found him crying last night, heartbroken because you might leave." Her shot had hit home.

Marie's eyes opened wide. Her voice was incredulous. "Bob? Bob cried? I've never seen him cry."

Camilla pressed her advantage. "He really cares, Mrs. Classon." On impulse she left her desk, walked around to the other woman, and put her hand on her shoulder. "Don't throw it away because of what he did. Once someone loved me, a great deal. I cared, too. Something happened, he didn't trust me. I wasn't able to forgive." Her throat closed, thinking of how it was all past tense. Over. Once upon a time, but no happily ever after.

Marie Classon was staring at her, her own problems forgotten in the awareness of pain within Camilla. "Miss Clark, what happened?"

"He is going to marry someone else."

She saw the involuntary pity in the older woman's eyes.

"I'm sorry."

Camilla continued. "Don't let your pride keep you from accepting his apology, Mrs. Classon."

When Marie stood, she seemed a foot taller than when she had come in the office. "Thank you, Miss Clark." Her look told Camilla it would be all right. "I'm going to Bob now and tell him I can hardly wait for him to get home." She was gone, leaving Camilla alone in the little office.

Why was it so easy to help others solve their problems, so hard to put into practice in her own life what she had said? If only she had dropped her pride and accepted Marc's apology. Now it was too late.

How could she go to him, tell him she had been wrong? She couldn't.

The Classons would find happiness again — all she had was misery, and it was her own fault.

Chapter 13

"Good-bye, Miss Clark — and thanks." Gratitude shone in Bob Classon's face. It was reflected in his wife's. They were in the car ready to go home. The final tests had been made. Camilla had been right. It was simply nervous tension, pressure that was causing the problems.

"Good-bye." She waved, thinking how nice it was to see a "happy ending." So many of her patients came and went. She only had contact with them while they were in the hospital and never got to meet their families.

She shrugged and turned back to her ward. It was part of the job. Maybe that's why it had made the Classons so special, the glimpse of home life, the opportunity to help.

If only someone would help her! Daily the hospital grapevine faithfully reported the new developments about Dr. Marc Butler. Speculation ran high as to who the woman was. Some said it was an old girlfriend from California. Others sagely shook their heads, insisting it was someone he'd met in Auburn. Still others frankly admitted they didn't know, but with all the fixing up, it couldn't be long.

Where the first rumor started that it was to be a June wedding, no one knew. Did it stem from the fact Dr. Butler had asked for a two-week vacation then? Camilla didn't know or care. All she knew was that the days were spinning past, madly racing toward a time when her private world would shatter.

Marc Butler's wedding day would also be the day her career as head nurse on ward 8 of the Auburn Veterans' Hospital ended. She wouldn't stay, not with him married to someone else. If it was cowardly to run, then she was a coward of the first order.

She wasn't strong enough to run into him now and then, knowing she had thrown away something very precious, something that might have been.

"Camilla, would you stop by my office before going off duty?" Alice's voice came over the phone, crisp and efficient. There was no place in the director of nurses' position for the softer, more loving Alice Montgomery Camilla knew at home.

Her heart jumped every time she saw Alice and Jim together. As had been predicted, he walked stiffly, but he did walk. There wasn't a day that passed without

Camilla giving thanks for Jim's partial recovery and for Alice.

There was nothing in Alice's voice to betray she was part of a conspiracy as she greeted Camilla. "Sit down, Camilla. How did your shift go?"

"Fine."

Alice saw how very tired Camilla looked. It strengthened her in what she planned to do. Not even the hospital director knew of a certain doctor's visit to Alice. The result was what would take place now.

"I'm working on vacation schedules. I'd like to schedule you for the last two weeks in June. Is that all right with you?"

Camilla started. The last two weeks in June? What a strange coincidence. That was when Dr. Butler would be off.

"It's just that usually during the summer, people want off all at once and I'll need you then. Besides, you never did get your spring vacation. I think a couple weeks away from here will do you good."

Camilla didn't see the compassion in Alice's eyes. She only thought of how ironic it was, having the same time off that Dr. Butler would be spending on his honeymoon, somewhere.

It worked right into her plans. She would take the time off, secure another job, and go right to it. Under the circumstances they'd let her go without too much notice, she was sure. Although Jim and Alice didn't discuss Dr. Butler in front of her, they were bound to wonder what had happened. Both had been so sure Marc loved her.

"That would be fine." Her voice was flat. It was the best she could do. "Anything else?"

"Not unless you have something for me." It was an open invitation for confidences, but Camilla found herself reluctant to put in words all the fears and plans she had tentatively made. Time enough for all that later. Then almost without her knowing why, she blurted out, "Have you seen Dr. Butler's quarters? I understand he is really fixing them up."

Alice didn't let on there was anything other than idle curiosity behind the question. "Yes, I have. He's really making them beautiful. You know, they were all done before the hospital opened. Well, he's kept the best of those furnishings and added a lot of his own. He's relying heavily on yellows, golds, and oranges."

She looked at Camilla speculatively. "He commented on how well he liked what you'd done to our home. Any chance of your helping him out? You're better with color than I am, and he was wishing he had someone to help him with the final decisions."

For a moment Camilla thought she would burst into hysterical laughter. Alice was asking *her* to help Dr. Butler furnish his quarters — for an unknown bride? It was followed by another thought. If she'd even fooled Alice these last weeks, maybe the rest of the hospital didn't know of the king-size torch she was carrying for the good doctor.

A curious smile touched her lips and she looked straight at Alice. "That would be very nice. Do you want to tell him?"

Alice had all she could do to keep from giving away everything she knew or surmised. She wanted to stand and cheer at the strength of the slim girl in the white uniform looking at her so steadily. Instead, she merely nodded. "I'll let him know. He can get in touch with you and set a time."

"Fine." Camilla stepped toward the door. "We who are about to die salute you." Where had that bit of prose come from? She didn't even remember who had said it or why. The next moment she was walking down the hall, through the front doors, and across the street. Reaction didn't set in until she reached the haven of her own room, quiet, removed from all her earthly problems.

What had she done? She saw herself in the mirror, pale as an Ice Maiden. She had promised to help Dr. Butler decide on final choices for his redecorating. Wasn't it the best way to let the hospital grapevine know there was nothing between her and Dr. Butler, and never would be?

What was in the past could stay buried. She'd carry on, even attend his wedding if she were invited. Then she'd run far away and hide herself where she could lick her wounds. No one would ever be able to connect her with Marc Butler. One more thing, she would never, ever trust or love another man so long as she lived. Mr. Right had turned out wrong. But she wanted no other.

It was remarkable what a strong decision could do, Camilla thought. New strength flowed through her. Once she had decided on her course, things seemed to fall into place. She wasn't the first woman to lose the man she loved. She wouldn't be the last. She chuckled. There was something in that old adage about misery loving company.

"Here's to you, Camilla!" She raised her hairbrush in mock salute to the imaged girl. No more weeping in the pillow for her. She was a nurse, a professional, trained to work with people. She would be true to her calling. If she couldn't have happiness herself, she would bring it to others. In time a certain contentment would replace the fiery protest inside her. She would find peace.

Camilla thought of Alice, true to Jim and her love for all those years. For a moment she wavered. Then the determined chin went up; the eyes opened wide. She and Alice were two different people.

There was only one more thing to face. She owed an apology to Marc Butler. So he was marrying someone else. She still burned with shame to think how ungraciously she had accepted his sincere regrets. She had been flippant, rude, gauche. If she let things slide, never mentioned it again, there would always be this splinter in her conscience. She couldn't live with that.

"I'll do it." Her wave to her reflection was a promise. "When he has me look over his color scheme, I'll apologize. Very quietly, without any dramatics. I was good in acting in high school. Now I can see just how good. I'll put on an act that leaves Marc Butler respecting me, maybe even regretting he found someone else so quickly. It's the only way." Her smile deepened, showing two dimples. "Who knows? I might even grow up after all!"

The smile lingered through dinner. Jim and Alice eyed her suspiciously. It was the first time they'd seen her so lighthearted in a long time.

Jim finally asked her bluntly, "Who gave you the world on a string?"

Camilla's face was innocent, her eyes devilish. "Alice did."

"I!" Alice stared at her. Had Camilla somehow found out . . . ?

"Sure. You told me I get my vacation early this summer. Isn't that enough to make anyone happy?" She didn't see how Alice relaxed or the exchange of glances between her and Jim.

"Good to have your old self back, Cam." Jim's gruff voice brought stinging tears to her eyes. She hadn't realized how much her troubles had rubbed off on Jim.

"You see before you a new woman!"

"New woman, why don't you buy some new clothes to go with your vacation? Do you know where you're going?" Alice was surprised by the turn of events. Had she been wrong? Well, she had given her word. She'd carry on.

"No, not yet. But that's a good idea. Off with the old, on with the new." The looks on their faces made Camilla laugh. "I feel positively giddy!"

"Better go shopping with her, Alice," Jim advised. "I don't think she's to be trusted in this mood."

Their shopping expedition proved to be a huge success. Although, as Camilla said when she got home, "I almost bought enough for a complete trousseau." She looked accusingly at Alice. "You were supposed to tone me down. Instead, you urged me to buy everything I liked. Just look at that!"

She waved at the bed and open closet. "Dresses, dresses everywhere, plus lingerie, plus shoes, plus sports clothes. Were we both insane?"

Alice refused to be tempted into an argument. Things had gone exactly the way she had hoped. "Don't forget. Just because you wear uniforms most of the time here doesn't mean you won't need good clothing for your vacation. You hadn't really cleaned out your closet for several years. A lot of the things are the wrong length, or style. Give the Salvation Army a break and donate some of your old stuff." She busied herself pulling out clothes. "Here, can I help?"

"Sure."

In moments they had stacked Camilla's old clothing into two piles: "keep" and "give away."

"What about this?" Alice held up a red pantsuit.

Camilla swallowed hard to cover the emotion the sight of that pantsuit brought. It was what she'd worn the night she met Dr. Butler. "Keep it. It's one of my favorites." Inside she was scolding, *You should get rid of it. It will only bring back memories.*

But she couldn't do it. She would keep it and someday wear it and smile over the girl she had been, waiting for her Mr. Right.

Alice pretended not to notice Camilla's reaction. "If I were you, I wouldn't wear any of the new things until my vacation. That way it will seem all fresh, bright, everything different."

"Good idea. I'll get everything packed in the next week or so. It isn't long until June."

"No, it isn't." Alice's voice was deliberately casual. "By the way, did Dr. Butler get in touch with you?"

"Yes. I'm going over tomorrow afternoon and look at his house." She didn't add that when Marc called, her fingers trembled even though she had kept her voice steady. "He said he wanted to get it all finished before — before he went on vacation."

She seemed so cool. Alice shot a sidelong glance at her. What if she had been wrong about Camilla? A trickle of fear went through Alice, leaving her feeling as if she'd stepped into an icy shower. Camilla would never forgive her. Well, it was too late now.

She was committed to follow through the plan she had agreed on.

"All finished." Alice made her voice cheerful. "When Jim gets home, you'll have to show him your new things. That's one of the traits I like about him. He's always interested in what I wear."

Jim Montgomery wasn't thinking of spring clothes at that moment. He was facing a dark-haired, determined doctor across the desk in his office. "I think it's preposterous, that's what I think!"

"Do you? You must know how I feel, how I've felt ever since I came. Do you have any objection?"

"No, I don't. I would have before you came here. No more. If you insist on this, then that's the way it will be." A smile broke through the craggy features. The blue eyes twinkled. "I'll even wish you good luck. But what Camilla is going to think when she hears all this, I shudder to consider."

The tall man stood. "Why not let me worry about that? If you'll just do as I asked, I'll take care of the rest."

Two strong hands met across the desk. There was strength in the clasp. Then the tall man left the room, while Jim Montgomery stayed to consider everything that had passed between them. He had to admit, it was just crazy enough to work. But as he slowly made his way home, again his mind asked, *What is Camilla going to think?*

There was a fashion show at the Montgomery home that evening. Alice was right. Jim was always interested in what they wore. As Camilla paraded around in her new garments, Jim watched her with pride. Surely things couldn't be so bad if she could look like that! It helped salve his conscience.

When the show was over, Jim sprawled in his big chair, watching his sister. "Now that you have the wardrobe, where are you going to take it?"

"I don't know. Got any ideas?"

It was the opening for which he'd been angling. "Matter of fact, I do. There was some literature in the office today about a cruise up to Alaska. I've never seen more beautiful scenery. How would you like something like that?" He didn't dare look directly at her.

"Alaska! Alaska? What on earth would I do on a cruise to Alaska?" She was incredulous.

"You could relax." There was something in Jim's voice that stopped her short. "You need to get away. There are always charming people on cruises. It would be good for you. Get you in a land of beautiful mountains, rivers, and lakes. Give you a fresh outlook."

"You really want me to go, don't you?"

"You can't know how much." That was the understatement of the year. Jim grimaced, thinking of what to say next. He didn't have to say anything.

Camilla understood that for some reason this was important to him. The more she thought of it, the more it appealed to her. She'd always wanted to visit Alaska but hadn't thought the chance would come so soon. "All right. But isn't it a bit late to get reservations?"

This was the crucial moment. Jim caught up a newspaper for a shield as he told her, "Oh, they were made quite some time ago."

"What?" She marched over and took down the paper from in front of his face. "You mean to tell me you made reservations for me before you even asked if I'd go? Of all the officious, high-handed —"

"Brotherly," he inserted smoothly. "Go ahead and sputter. If I'd waited until you agreed to make reservations, you probably wouldn't be going."

"And if I had preferred to spend my vacation with people I knew?" He disregarded the ominous tone. "Oh, I knew you'd enjoy this particular cruise."

The blandness of his voice smoothed her ruffled feathers. "All right, you win." She appealed to Alice. "Did you ever see such a bossy man?"

She got no support from Alice. "I agree with him, Camilla. You're going to love this cruise. You'll remember it as long as you live."

What was there in Alice's words to make her look like a cat who'd been in the cream? Camilla looked up suspiciously but couldn't see anything out of the way.

"I suppose that's why you insisted I buy so many new clothes. I suppose you two had it all planned out ahead of time." She flounced out the door, but stuck her head back in. "One of these days I'm going to plot against you, and look out!"

She disappeared down the hall into her own room. But her last waking thoughts were not of a trip to Alaska, but of an apology she had to make the next afternoon.

Chapter 14

Camilla slid her clothing along the rod. What should she wear? She wanted something to impress Marc Butler. An imp of perversity caused her hand to stop at the red pantsuit. Did she dare? Why not? It was almost too warm outside for such an outfit, but she didn't care. If she was going to apologize, she'd do it in style.

Never in her life had she dressed with such care. Every shining strand of her dark hair was in place. Her lipstick was perfect. She surveyed the girl in the mirror. Too pale. She never wore makeup except lipstick, so now she pinched her cheeks to give them color. That was better.

"Look out, Dr. Butler!" The smile she gave herself lingered as she walked down the hall to the living room.

Marc was already there. He'd told her he would stop by for her. It wasn't far to his quarters. They could walk it together.

"I really appreciate your taking the time to help me, Miss Clark." He sounded as if he had just met her, not like the man with whom she had shared such intense moments. It provided the final strengthening touch for Camilla.

"I hope your fiancee won't object." Darn! She hadn't meant to mention the fiancee until he did, then act cool about it.

Marc looked at her from the corner of his eyes. "Oh, she won't mind. She knows quite a lot about you."

Camilla came within a hair's breadth of stopping in the path and refusing to go on. Just what had he told this unknown fiancee? She recovered herself. Now was no time to turn chicken. She had a selling job to do, the biggest of her life. Nothing was going to stop her from carrying it through. Nothing!

If Marc Butler remembered another walk around the hospital, one that had taken place when snow was on the ground, and had ended in their monstrous misunderstanding, he gave no sign.

His face was lighted up. Camilla felt a pang of jealousy for the woman who could make him look like that. For most of the time she'd known him, he was either frowning at her or ignoring her. What would it be like to really be loved by him?

On the other hand, maybe it wouldn't be so special after all. If he could swear he loved her, yet within just a few days find someone else, it could have happened after marriage instead of before.

She shut down her memory track and hard. This was no time for speculation. Her voice was cool, her manner in perfect control. "Will you be staying with the hospital after your marriage, Dr. Butler?"

"Of course. I can't imagine working anywhere else. Your brother has done an outstanding job. I'd like to work here the rest of my life."

So would I, Camilla thought. *But I can't. Not with you here married to some woman who probably isn't even good enough for you.* An uncontrollable desire to find out more, perhaps even torture herself a little, caused her to ask, "What's she like? Your fiancee, I mean?"

A little smile played around the usually stern lips. Laughter danced in the dark eyes as Marc faced her. "Well, she's pretty hard to explain. She's about your size. She's —" He spread his hands helplessly. "How can you describe someone you love?"

Camilla forced words past the big lump in her throat. "I suppose she is sweet and gentle, doesn't have a temper."

"N-no. I wouldn't say that. Let's just say she's the only woman I could ever love for all my life. I can never get over being thankful I found her. Others may jump from love to love, but not me. I guess I'm old-fashioned, a one-woman man."

Camilla couldn't hold it back. "In spite of the act you put on pretending to love me?" Her face burned. How could she have been so crude?

Marc laughed. "Maybe someday you'll understand about that." He shrugged his shoulders. "Those things happen, you know."

Camilla gritted her teeth. It was bad enough to have to listen to all his ravings about being true to his dream woman. To stand there and hear him brush off everything that had gone between them was practically the last straw. All her training came to her rescue. She would see this through. Then she'd never see this arrogant man again, never!

"Come in, Miss Clark." She didn't notice the unsteadiness of the strong hand opening the door for her, ushering her into his quarters. It was the beginning of a tour she would never forget.

"You'll see I've stuck to the autumn tones. My fiancee likes them. Now, what I'm wondering is —" He led the way into the living room. A fire was laid, ready for the touch of a match. Andirons gleamed. Books in shelves on either side of the fireplace looked inviting. Easy chairs beckoned.

Marc didn't seem to see how unstrung she was growing. "I'm trying to decide between these three fabrics for drapes." He held up a splashy white with orange flowers and green leaves, a muted plaid, and a plain ivory.

Camilla forced herself to feign interest. "Oh, the ivory. The others have too much color for this room."

"Good! I favored that myself, but the salesman insisted I bring the other samples."

It was just a start. From room to room they went: the blue and white kitchen just crying out for a homemaker's touch; the dining room with its maple furnishings and deep gold walls accented by white trim; the bedrooms, one rose, the other in shades of blue; the bathrooms, green, white, and gleaming. There were unexpected touches of yellows and oranges here and there, tying it all together.

"Well, I guess that's all." She was in the hall. Her fixed smile felt thin at the edges. "I guess I had better go."

"Thanks, Miss Clark." Dr. Butler was holding both her hands, beaming. "You'll never know how much I appreciate your helping me with these final touches."

Camilla knew, if she didn't get out of there, she was going to either laugh, scream, or cry. It was all too much. But there was one thing more she had to do. Summoning all her courage, she smiled up at him. "By the way, now that you are getting married and all, I don't want any hard feelings between us. I'd like to apologize for the way I acted at the warehouse. I do appreciate your helping Jim, and helping me remember. I don't want you to think I hold anything against you. The past is gone. I'd like to think we can be friends in the future."

The silence deepened until she felt it would never end. The two hands holding her own tightened. "I don't want you for a friend, Camilla Clark." Marc Butler's features looked chiseled. "It's far too late for that."

With a wrench she freed herself, her eyes cold. "Fine with me. I owed you an apology and you have it. I'll be leaving now. Congratulations and all that." She reached for the doorknob, only to be stopped as Marc stepped between her and the door.

"What are you doing?" She didn't heed the warning light in his eyes. When she saw it, she stepped back. It was too late.

The next moment he had her in his arms,

kissing her the way he had done before. She was stunned. Why would Marc Butler kiss her now? He had said he didn't want her for a friend. How dared he kiss her like this? She fought the impulse to put her head on his shoulder and cry the buckets of tears inside. Instead she jerked back.

"And I suppose this is being true to your fiancee, the woman you will love all your life! How will you explain that?"

"I won't have to. She'll understand, in time." He ignored the angry rush of color to her face. "I had to detain you, Miss Clark. I want you to meet my fiancee." He glanced at the clock. "Good. You can meet her in just a few minutes."

"You fiancee is going to be here?" Camilla could feel her voice getting dangerously high. "She's in town? Then why did you bring me here? Why didn't she select her own furnishings? What kind of game are you playing?"

"The most important one of my life." Marc grasped her by the shoulders. "I told you that when someone saves your life, then you belong to them by right of salvage. I meant it. I also told you I might go caveman and drag you off." He forced a laugh. "Well, I thought better of that, but I did decide to get you here and make you listen to sense for once in your life. You are going to walk into that living room and meet my fiancee, and you are going to do it now!"

Good heavens, had the woman slipped in while they were upstairs? Camilla felt herself propelled into the living room. Her eyes looked around. The room was empty.

"Where is she?" There was no use struggling against his hard grip. He marched her to the mantel, forcing her to look straight ahead. "Right there!"

She gasped. Above the mantel was a large mirror, reflecting the room. It also reflected two people: a tall, dark-haired man who looked furious; a dark-eyed, colorless girl in a red pantsuit.

For a moment the two reflections looked back. Then she felt Marc's fingers loosen. She nearly fell, but managed to drop into a chair. "You mean — me? I'm the fiancee?"

"That's right."

"Are you crazy? I haven't said I'd marry you!" She ignored the wild surge of elation inside, the knowledge of freedom. There was no other fiancee, Marc Butler loved her!

"You will." He was cocksure, supremely confident. It was too much for her. She got to her feet, walked to the doorway. "That's what you think. I'm going home where I belong."

He didn't make a move. His voice stopped her effectively. "That's where you are, Camilla. You're home where you belong."

The quietness of his voice steadied her whirling brain. "Then all along, all the hospital grapevine, the remodeling, everything —" A new suspicion sprang to life. "Alice. Scheduling me for a June vacation. She knew?"

Marc's eyes opened wide. "Of course. I couldn't very well ask for time off for you without telling her."

Camilla was still having trouble believing it. "This is some horrible joke, some revenge. You're all in it together!"

"No, Camilla. It was the only way I could think of to break down the barrier you'd put between us. Actually, it was the barrier I raised by my lack of trust. It had to come down. This was the only way."

With a final spurt of hurt pride and independence she said, "I don't think I can marry anyone who is so underhanded."

It brought Marc to her. "And how would you have suggested I do it, my dear girl? Like this?"

This time his kiss was welcomed, returned. It left her shaken. It was real. He loved her, he'd always love her. With a sigh she gave in, leaned against him, heard the beating of his heart.

"We have a few things to plan." He led her back to the big chair and sat on its arm. "A honeymoon, for instance."

"Honeymoon!" Camilla returned to reality from the future dream world she had been inhabiting. "Marc, I'm signed up for a two-week Alaskan cruise the last part of June."

"I know. I made our reservations weeks ago."

"You *what?*"

"Are you growing deaf, Camilla? I made our reservations weeks ago."

"Then Jim was in on it, too." She glared at him. "And I suppose that's why Alice insisted I buy all those new clothes, and why they were going to ship me off to Alaska, and —" Her face burned with color remembering what Alice had said.

"And what?" His voice was low, amused.

"Alice said I'd love this cruise. That — that I'd remember it as long as I lived."

She was greeted with a shout of laughter from Marc.

"I certainly intend to see that you do." He watched her growing confusion, hesitated, then added, "Don't be embarrassed, Camilla. We weren't so sure as we pretended. I didn't know you would feel you had to apologize today. If you hadn't, I would never have let you leave until I'd told you the truth."

He gathered her into his arms again. "I meant it when I said you were the only woman in the world I could have loved for all time."

The sincerity in his voice settled her more than anything else could have done. "Marc, I once told Jim that when my Mr. Right came along, nothing on earth would stand in my way. I didn't know how much would get in the way!"

She raised her eyes to his. "No more. One thing, we won't have to fight when we get married. We've done enough of it already to get it out of our systems."

He laughed at that, holding her even closer. "Can you be ready to be married in just a few days?"

"A few days. Why?"

"I hate to have these go to waste." He reached around her for a box on the table. It was full of white envelopes. "Open one."

Wonderingly she ran a finger beneath a flap. Inside was a printed card:

Mr. and Mrs. James Montgomery announce the wedding of Camilla Clark, R.N., and Marc Butler, M.D., on June 15, 1980

"Wedding announcements? All printed?"

"We thought that Camilla Clark, R.N., might not want to see Marc Butler, M.D., humiliated after the notices were all ready to go out."

With a tender look Marc put the card back in the box. "You don't really mind, do you, Camilla? Alice said, when she was married so simply in the hospital chapel, you told her if you ever got married you'd like it that way. No fuss and feathers. No getting the bride worn out with shopping and showers and picking silver patterns.

"I love you, Camilla. Will you marry me on June 15th and let Jim and Alice send out the cards? We won't have time. We'll be on our way to Alaska."

It was the perfect opportunity. It was perhaps the last opportunity she would ever have to get even with Marc, Jim, and Alice. Camilla dropped her eyelashes. "Well, I hate to see money wasted on useless wedding announcements . . ."

"And?"

"And since I already have picked out the furnishings for this place and . . ."

"And?"

"And since I was already scheduled for the Alaskan cruise, a honeymoon shouldn't interfere too much with my plans."

"Camilla!" She looked up at the stern

command in his eyes. "None of those reasons are valid. There's only one reason for you to accept my proposal."

In spite of her rapid heartbeat, she couldn't help but be a little jubilant over his response.

"You know that we will have differences, Cam. We are two separate people. Yet we can have joy in sharing, in working together, in building a life. Only those who love one another with all their hearts can win in the marriage game. Unless you feel as I do, I don't want you. I'd rather go throughout life alone than settle for second best." There was an unaccustomed twist to his lips, a sweetness mixed with determination.

For a moment Camilla closed her eyes, remembering back to another Marc who had stood in a hospital room, accepting a challenge to make her brother's dream come true. She thought of what he had given up, his way of life as a rich man's son, his own plans if he had had any. That careless boy was gone forever. The man he had become was asking her to be his wife, to share everything, through better or worse.

"I will be honored to be your wife. I will love and cherish you as long as I live." She would make her wedding vows later, but no moment would stand out more clearly than this one.

This time Marc's kiss was gentle, tender. When it was over, she leaned back from him. "If you'll take me home, I have a wedding dress to buy and packing for a certain cruise to do."

He looked at her, radiant in the same red pantsuit she had worn when he first met her. It was still almost more than he could believe. Camilla would be his wife in just a few days.

"Woman!" His voice was thrillingly gruff. "When you pack for your honeymoon, don't forget to put in that red pantsuit."

Her eyes met his, memories stirring in them both. "Yes, sir." She saluted smartly and marched toward the door. But there was nothing military in the look she gave Marc. It was made of the deep love she had fought so long — and promise for the future now waiting.